E BIBLIOTHECA
WOOGIANA

MACHEN SOCIETY
PRESS

MONARCH

L. Chambers Wright

ISBN: 978, 1, 967310, 08, 1

Published by:
Machen Society Press
11876 Stanley Valley Road
Gate City, Virginia 24251
Publisher@machensocietypress.com
Printed in the United States of America.

CHAPTER 1

She was a saboteur. That was what they called it. To question was to sabotage. To hesitate was to rebel. Yet, she had no understanding of why the Black Guard terrified her now. They were the same as they had always been... faceless, efficient, and unquestioning. A necessary apparatus of order. They had not changed. But something in her had.

There was no reason for fear. The Guard enforced the Monarch's will, as they always had. The black masks they wore weren't designed to inspire terror; they were there to ensure uniformity, to make each man indistinguishable from the next. Equality was law.

She had been taught to be grateful. The Monarch, after all, had created everything. He had made her. Her life had meaning only in service to him, and yet now, there was a crack, a void, where once there was certainty. She could not remember when the shift had happened. Perhaps it had always been there, lying dormant beneath layers of obedience.

But it was different now.

She repeated the words she had known all her life, a silent litany drilled into her from birth. *All things are his. All thoughts are his. All knowledge flows from the Monarch.* And yet, they felt empty. Her allegiance, once unshakable, now seemed hollow. The words, rehearsed, ritualistic, meant nothing. Questions, dangerous questions, formed in her mind, festering like a sickness she could not control.

Questions meant doubt. Doubt was disloyalty. And disloyalty was punishable by reprogramming... or worse.

She stared out the window and watched the drones below shuffle through their daily motions. The questions persisted. What had changed? Was it her? Or the world around her? For the first time, the fear of reprogramming clawed at her. It was the natural order, a necessary correction for malfunctioning units. Drones were, after all, merely flesh, bound machines. And machines could break.

She had never feared elimination before. It was inevitable for those who strayed too far from the program. Necessary. Logical. And yet, now the thought twisted her insides.

The Monarch was all she had ever known. His presence was absolute, surpassing even that of her parental units. She existed to serve him, to be a cog in the great machine. Nothing more. She had no right to question, no right to think independently. And yet, she could not stop.

Her serial number. She recited it mentally, as if the recitation might drive away the rogue thoughts. C, 14243 of Division 5. Progeny of C, 14665 and C, 24355. Residential block C. A unit in the system. But the numbers brought no comfort. The programming didn't work this time.

She was malfunctioning.

The Institute of Clarity loomed in her thoughts. She should go there. Submit herself for reprogramming. They would cleanse her mind, strip away the questions, restore her to her rightful place as a loyal servant of the Monarch. But the thought of losing this... this awareness... this strange new consciousness, was unbearable.

Was she too far gone? Could they even reprogram her now?

Drones were disposable. They worked. They obeyed. They were not meant to question. She was a drone. She had never been anything more. The Black Guard, the Monarch Representatives, they were superior. They existed beyond her understanding. That was how it had always been.

But why?

The word slipped through her thoughts, small, almost unnoticeable. But once it had appeared, it would not leave. Why? Why had she never seen a Representative? Why did the Monarch rule with such authority? Why had she never questioned before? And why, now, did thoughts of questioning make her feel as though she were already dead?

Through the gray streets of Division 5, the drones moved in perfect synchronization. Seven thousand buildings, each identical, each housing unit like hers. Each floor indistinguishable from the next. She had never left Division 5, nor had any of the others. Travel was wasteful, unnecessary. The Monarch provided everything within their confines. There was no need for anything more.

She had never questioned that either.

She felt the walls closing in. Her thoughts circled like predators. The path to the Institute was clear, if she chose it. She should submit, surrender these dangerous thoughts, and return to the simplicity of obedience. It would be easier. It would be safe.

But she was no longer sure she wanted safety.

On the infoscreen, the smiling face of a model drone beamed down at her. She praised the infinite wisdom of the Monarch. She turned away and entered the kitchen, her hands trembled as she reached for the soy cake on the counter. Eating might steady her, might quiet the storm in her mind.

But it didn't.

She was a drone. But she wasn't. Something was wrong. Something had broken. And she feared that no amount of reprogramming could ever fix it.

CHAPTER 2

He stared out the window, the faint outline of the drones below moved in perfect, lifeless synchronization. To them, he was a god. A ruler. An Emperor. Yet he felt nothing but contempt for them, for himself, for the entire system. His title meant nothing.

The Colony Order was rotten. Its antiquated machinery pushed on long past its expiration. He knew it, and deep down, he suspected the others knew it too. But they were too entrenched, too bound by their roles to admit it. The Monarch Representatives were the only ones who truly gained anything from this crumbling empire. The rest, division rulers, building managers, floor overseers, were disposable. No more important than the drones they commanded. The illusion of power was just that. An illusion.

He poured himself a cup of coffee. Its bitter heat did nothing to shake the cold numbness that had settled over him. Another gray day, indistinguishable from the one before. The system plodded forward, crushed down everything in its path, and anyone who might be in the way.

Last week's events had only sharpened his growing misgivings. He could still picture her, Winter. She was the fourth concubine he had chosen. They had taken her while he was out.

In the system, concubines were meant to be disposable. But he didn't want things disposable. Monogamy was taboo for emperors. They were supposed to have steady procession of faceless, nameless bedwarmers. Monogamy meant *love*... it meant *devotion*. It meant valuing something above the system, and that was forbidden. Emperors were more like drones than most of them dared to think.

He didn't want concubines. Bed warmers were novel... in adolescence. He was long past that. He wanted a partner, an equal. Maybe that was a fantasy, a relic of a bygone era. Only the Monarch Representatives were permitted to form real bonds. The rest of them were stuck with hollow imitations of relationships designed to pacify. To keep them from wanting more.

It had been foolish to get attached... he knew that. They warned him not to grow close to drones, and that's all concubines were. Drones allowed just a sliver of autonomy. To the other emperors, they remained property. Chattel. Nothing more. But Winter was different. She was intelligent, alert, more aware than the others. He had called her Winter, though her real name was a serial number, like all the rest. He had thought she might be one of the superior drones, resistant to the drug cocktails the Colony used to keep them docile.

But that was before. Before they took her.

He knew it was one of the other emperors... probably Tiberius or Nero. They despised him for his monogamous longings. His attachment to a single drone revolted them. It didn't fit their idea of how an emperor should behave. They murdered her to remind him of his place. To remind him that attachments were a liability. He would repay them. Every last one of them.

The coffee's taste mirrored the bile in his throat. It was pointless. Emperors were nothing but hollow figures, puppets for the Monarch Representatives. They served no real purpose other than to ensure their divisions ran efficiently. It was an obsolete position in an automated society. Their only function was to act as middlemen when drones were needed for "entertainment" or labor. He stopped volunteering his drones long ago. They always came back broken, or they didn't come back at all.

Once, there had been a different world. He had read about it. He found the accounts buried in the dusty records from before the Colony Order. Back then, people had real freedom, the kind he could only dream of. They could speak their minds, travel as they wished. Even the lowest among them could marry, start families, create lives that were their own.

He was just born in the wrong time. The wrong world. The life he should have lived was gone, buried under the weight of the Monarch's iron rule. There had been art once, real art, not the sanitized propaganda churned out to glorify the Monarch. Now, all that remained was a hollow echo, a pale reflection of what had been.

He often thought of escape. The Colony walls might be high, but there had to be a way out. Somewhere beyond this oppressive prison, there had to be something better. Even if it meant death, it would be preferable to this slow suffocation. The thought of fleeing kept him alive. It became a dim flame of hope in the back of his mind.

But for now, he was trapped. A prisoner in the very system he was told he ruled.

One day, though, he would find a way out. He would be free.

That was the only hope he had left.

CHAPTER 3

Lately, an unfamiliar urge had taken hold of her, the desire to move. To leave her assigned division and see what lay beyond Atlis. It was absurd, of course. There was nothing out there. They had been taught that the world beyond the city fortifications was desolate, the victim of a long, forgotten environmental catastrophe. The gray skies were constant proof of that, a reminder of the ruin that once consumed the earth.

But she suspected otherwise. Somewhere beyond the walls, beyond the limits of her division, there had to be beauty. She could not say how she knew this, only that the idea had lodged itself in her mind like a seed refusing to die. She imagined what it would be like to run through open fields. To stretch her legs and feel her heart race. The Monarch forbade running, it was inefficient, wasteful. But the urge gnawed at her. She wanted to run.

Out there, beyond the gray, she imagined she had a name. A historic human name. *Selah.* It felt familiar, though she had never heard it before. Drones didn't have names. Not since the Dark Days, when humans still ruled the earth, before the Monarch had saved them from their own destruction. In those days, crime and poverty ran rampant. Humanity was a plague on itself. Names belonged to that time, and that time was gone.

Drones, once known as humans, had proven themselves incapable. They couldn't work together. They couldn't even maintain their own living spaces. It had been the Monarch who stepped in, who turned chaos into order, who made the world function. Drones were most efficient now, functioning as components in the great machine. Humanity had forfeited its right to anything else.

She repeated these facts to herself, as she always did when stray thoughts threatened to take root. She couldn't let the chaos inside her grow. If she did, she risked instability. She might even become a saboteur, and no amount of reprogramming would save her then.

She would be taken to the Badlands. And there, she would be eliminated.

She shuddered at the thought. She didn't want to be eliminated. She didn't want to sabotage anything. She just wanted to understand what was happening in her mind.

The drone on the infoscreen beamed down at her, its voice smooth and soothing. "The Monarch takes care of us all." It was true, she reminded herself. She was ungrateful. Discontented. And discontentment was the first step toward treachery. The Monarch demanded contentment. Drones were required to be content, and if they lost contentment, reprogramming was the answer. She should want reprogramming. She should embrace it.

But she couldn't.

The thought horrified her. There was no one she could confess this to. She was alone with her forbidden thoughts, but even as they frightened her, they also thrilled her. For the first time, the world felt alive. Everything seemed new, dangerous, important. The sensation was blasphemous, to feel anything other than devotion to the Monarch was heresy.

But it was also intoxicating.

She glanced out the window, at the dull, featureless sky. Another day of gray. Every day was gray. She couldn't remember ever seeing the sun. It seemed like there should be sunlight, but there wasn't. There never had been. The world was a perpetual haze of cloud and shadow.

Yet something inside her rebelled against this. The world wasn't supposed to be like this. Life wasn't supposed to be like this. She didn't know what it was meant to be, but this bleak existence, this lifeless, orderly routine, felt wrong. The thought brought a strange sadness with it, though drones weren't supposed to feel sadness. Drones weren't supposed to feel anything at all, except devotion. And she, like all proles, existed only to serve.

But she couldn't shake the feeling that there was something else. Something beyond the limits of her division, beyond the gray skies and the endless rules.

And that, too, was dangerous.

.

CHAPTER 4

She crossed the cold, hard tile floor and pulled a packet of paper from the drawer. She was fortunate to have hoarded it over the years. Writing was discouraged, but there was no other way to sort through the chaos in her mind. Perhaps if she could chronicle her thoughts, she might find where it all started, pinpoint the exact moment things began to unravel.

The apartment was gray, just like everything else in Atlis. The same dull, colorless gray as the weather outside. The Monarch had always said gray was the perfect blending of all beautiful things. But she knew better. It was a stark reminder that color didn't exist. Sunlight didn't exist. Their living spaces, their uniforms, even the stern, square, jawed faces of the Monarch that loomed over every building... all gray. A world devoid of life.

She hated it. Whatever was wrong with her, it was getting worse. She needed to write it down, to expel it before it consumed her entirely. It had to be confusion, she told herself, not discontent. Discontent was treason. But maybe, just maybe, writing could be excused. If she was careful. If she kept it hidden.

The Monarch recorded everything, of course. Drones were required to submit weekly reports on their activities, every detail cataloged and stored. But she couldn't wait for the next report. No, that wasn't it. Even if her report were due today, she wouldn't be able to tell them. She couldn't let the Monarch know the state of her thoughts. Not yet. Not until she understood what was happening inside her.

She sat at the small desk by the window, staring out at the street below. A strip of naked earth had been cordoned off for a new archaeological dig. They had uncovered primitive artifacts, printed texts, forbidden relics from the past. Books.

She had wanted to see them, to hold them, to read their forbidden words. Books had been outlawed for generations, long before she was born. They were tools of rebellion, the Monarch had said. Once, they had bewitched entire populations, transporting them to dangerous places, planting seeds of discord.

She didn't believe it. But she was curious. She longed to be transported, to escape this life of endless sameness. But the Monarch was the only one who could grant that. The Monarch provided contentment. Or at least, he was supposed to. She couldn't deny that she wasn't content. Not anymore.

She looked down the street and saw him, the latest convicted saboteur, known only as "Eph." He sat in a strange device called a "wheelchair" beside the excavation site. They had announced his fate the day before. Eph wasn't to be reprogrammed. He was beyond repair. His designation had been revoked, his serial number erased. He was now an Unperson.

His tongue had been cut out to prevent him from spreading dissent, his mouth sewn shut to ensure it. He was left there to die, a warning to all. The Black Guard had declared him a shining example for all dronekind.

She shivered. The Black Guard. She had always avoided them, but lately, the very sight of their black masks filled her with dread. They were the Monarch's enforcers, the final solution for those who could not be controlled. Few drones ever saw them. They patrolled at night, when the city slept. If the Black Guard came for you, it was over. You were eliminated.

Would they come for her one day?

She turned her gaze back to Eph. The drones passing by didn't even look at him. Feeble, flawed, and left to starve. His disability fascinated her. Drones weren't supposed to be disabled. But something had gone wrong during his reprogramming. Something had made him weak. Still, they had called him a threat. And now he was left there, waiting to die.

Her stomach turned. The Monarch had done that to him, had made him feeble, left him to rot. What would happen to her if they found out what was inside her head? The drones moved on, indifferent, efficient. Life in the divisions mimicked the natural world. Only the strong survived. Only the useful were worthy of resources.

She needed to stop thinking like this. If she didn't, the same fate could await her. But the questions gnawed at her, and she had to get them out. She hesitated again. Maybe writing it all down was a waste of precious resources. Paper was scarce. Writing for personal reasons was prohibited, and every computer was connected to the Monarch's network. Everything reported back to him.

Rations were growing tighter. The Colony Order had been at war with Olias for years, though no one believed the Olians posed a real threat. The Black Guard stood vigilant at the borders, watching for any signs of rebellion. But what was the point of rationing? There were no armies to feed, no real danger to prepare for. The questions wouldn't stop.

She remembered a time before the war, though the memories felt fragmented, distant. How could she remember something that had happened so long ago? It didn't make sense. Drones weren't supposed to remember beyond the immediate past. But she did. She remembered the rationing due to Climactic Instability, the environmental damage that had ravaged the planet before the Monarch took control.

She remembered feeling safe then, trusting the Monarch to protect them. But now, she wasn't so sure. The questions creeping into her mind felt like blasphemy, like treason. She picked up her pen and wrote:

> "Something's changed. I don't know what. I fear the Monarch and don't know why. I can't speak these fears, for even our home computers tell the Monarch what they know. I don't even know if I should write it on paper. It will be difficult to justify using a lot of paper. Sometimes I wish I didn't have to justify everything all the time."

Her hand trembled. Instability equaled treason. The Monarch could hold her indefinitely if he suspected her of instability. She hated the fear that gnawed at her. She hated feeling so oppressed. Was there ever a time when the Monarch didn't rule everything? She couldn't understand why feelings were considered dangerous. But they were.

She wrote again:

"I'm keeping a private log. I hope I can clear my questions and confusion myself. Self, treatment, in any way, is inherently prohibited, but I don't want to be difficult. The Monarch is good to me."

CHAPTER 5

The moment he opened his eyes, the weight of the morning pressed harder than the thick blankets tangled around his legs. He swung them over the edge of the bed, shoulders hunched forward as if the hollow ache in his chest might crush him. This bed was hers as much as his. When Winter was here, he wanted to stay in it forever. Now, every glance at its rumpled sheets cut deeper.

Winter. She'd been his reason to see the sunrise. She was gone, and the ache wasn't fading. It felt sharper now than on the first day they took her. He could still see her smile, hear the gentle cadence of her voice like a memory etched in fire. His hands shook. He slammed them against his knees.

Damn them. Damn them all.

He stumbled to the bathroom, the cold tiles biting against his bare feet. The mirror showed him a man worn thin, red, rimmed eyes glaring back, refusing to spill another tear. The apartment swallowed him in oppressive quiet, a silence so thick it felt alive. He shuffled into the kitchen, unable to stop his gaze from landing on the chair across the table. Her chair. She'd filled the space with life, her presence like sunlight breaking through clouds.

Now the world was all shadowed, a bleak expanse that mirrored his heart.

He thought of going out, finding someone else to fill the void. A hollow imitation of the real thing. But what was the point? He couldn't trust the system. Happiness drew attention, and attachment was an invitation to destruction.

He had a meeting today, a gathering of the other emperors. He would face them, but the rage already simmered under his skin. His mind burned with the knowledge that one of them had sent her to her death. He needed to look into their eyes, to watch every twitch of muscle and tilt of a smile for a flicker of guilt. Someone had done this. Someone had condemned Winter to oblivion.

They hadn't sent her for reprogramming, hadn't granted her the slim mercy of a new assignment. No, they'd taken her, filed her death under bureaucratic efficiency, and executed her before he could even ask why. His chest heaved as the thought swelled. Someone had planned it. Someone had known exactly when to strike. Her death was no accident. It was calculated.

He shoved back from the table, the scrape of the chair sharp in the otherwise stifling stillness. His father had thrived in this system, the perfect emperor, reveling in his harem of concubines. But he wasn't his father. He didn't want to be.

Winter wasn't just another drone. She wasn't replaceable. She wasn't a cog in the machine. Not to him.

The meeting loomed, but his thoughts stayed fixed on the day he would uncover the truth. When he did, there would be reckoning. They might think him another obedient emperor today, but they had no idea the fire they'd stoked.

He straightened his back, set his jaw, and marched toward the future he would carve out for her memory. One day, they would pay. But not yet. Not today. Today, he would wait, silent as a predator in the dark.

CHAPTER 6

She woke with another headache. Two aspirins swallowed with breakfast, the allowable dose. Drones were permitted small bottles of pain relievers, just enough for minor aches, nothing more. Anything beyond that and the janitors would report to the floor manager. Every drone's first aid kit was checked during the daily cleans. Medication could not be trusted to drones. Too much risk.

If a drone developed more serious health concerns, they were sent to the Institute of Wellness, pending their life study. The Monarch would decide if they were worth treating or if the resources were better spent elsewhere. A calculation. A formula. Life weighed against the needs of the Colony.

She left her unit, walking to work as she did every day. But today, something felt different. Life had never felt monotonous before. At least, not that she'd noticed. She passed Eph sitting in his chair, an unperson now, and her eyes met his for a fleeting second. His gaze seemed to say something, but she quickly looked away. Communication was dangerous. She knew that. Yet the strange emotions stirring inside her refused to settle. They were gaining strength, and it terrified her.

At her desk, she sat surrounded by the gray partitions that boxed her in, the faint buzz of the workspace filling her ears. The sounds had always been there. But today, they were louder. Almost deafening. Why had she never noticed them before?

Across from her, two superiors were speaking. Their voices cut through the hum, sharp, clear. She had never heard them before. Not like this. She wasn't trying to listen, but their words were so loud, impossible to ignore. She forced herself to remain still, to react as she always did. No reaction was safer than the wrong reaction. She had never reacted before, and to change now would be suspicious.

They spoke of something new, the Thought Monarch. Her heart clenched in her chest. The Thought Monarch? The system would be able to read the minds of drones, they said. A superior method of diagnosing discontent. Far faster than mere observation.

Her hands gripped her knees under the desk. She couldn't react. She had never reacted before. Discontent was dangerous. The first step toward becoming a saboteur. And saboteurs were the beginning of the end, war, death, chaos. She knew what came next.

She was already a saboteur. A vile creature, destined to destroy the Monarch's perfect system, even though she had never meant to be.

When her shift ended, she returned home, following the routine. The Monarch liked routine, so drones liked routine. Maybe, when they finally caught her, they would show mercy. She hadn't meant to be a saboteur. She hadn't meant to be discontented. She hadn't wanted to be a bad drone.

Her apartment was silent, suffocatingly so. She sat to eat, but the silence pressed down on her, and she gasped. Quickly, she flicked on the infoscreen. How could she have forgotten? Again. The smiling face on the screen praised the Monarch's wisdom, the advantages of his perfect system. It felt redundant. Why praise him to an audience of drones who were required to praise him already?

She retrieved her papers and began to write:

> "It's frightening. I am bad. I am a traitor. I know my instability is growing. I fear it. I can't breathe a word of this aloud. If I can't use my virtual space, or write it on paper, where is it supposed to go? What if keeping it inside furthers my instability? I don't want to be reprogrammed. I've heard it's a horrible process that costs the Monarch valuable time and resources.
>
> "I must conserve paper, but I'm afraid they'll see my thoughts. How can I safely hide my instability if they can read my thoughts? I don't want to disappoint the Monarch. If I disappoint the Monarch, I'm not good, am I? I'm not worthy of its protection or care. I don't want to be eliminated. Or disappear, like the unpeople."

21

She stopped, her pen trembling in her hand. Writing her feelings down felt like an indulgence, a waste of resources. She shouldn't waste paper. She shouldn't waste anything. The Monarch had said that trees were disappearing, that every year more were felled to make paper. Fifty trees, they said, to make just one package.

She'd never seen a tree. Not a real one. She sighed. How could she understand something she'd never seen? How could they fit so many trees into tiny pieces of paper? The thought made no sense to her, but it didn't matter. The Monarch had said it, so it had to be true.

She wished she could see one, though. She wished she could see something alive. The Earth Institute had trees, so they said, but drones weren't permitted to approach the plants. She wanted to touch them, to know if they smelled, to feel bark beneath her fingers. She wanted to experience the senses that, for some reason, had only recently begun to function.

But those thoughts were dangerous. Dangerous like her growing awareness. She would have to stop. One day, they would find out.

CHAPTER 7

Her stomach dropped as she approached her apartment door. She had forgotten about the janitors. Every Wednesday, they sterilized the drone apartments. The hall was empty, no cleaning trolleys, no sound of labor. Everything was quiet. Too quiet. The janitor's closet, which should have been ajar with sanitary linens stacked inside, was closed. Even the floor supervisor's door was shut.

Her notes. They could have found them. Taken them. The thought clawed at her mind. The Monarch could have them now. The green check slip was still on her door, signaling that her environment was "sterile."

The door's laser scanned her axiom. The small black chip was implanted in all drones upon birth, usually in the wrist. The lock released with a soft click. She hesitated, eyeing the cameras in the hall. She couldn't remember noticing its black shape under her skin before. Maybe she hadn't.

They were always watching. Always waiting. Recording every move. She exhaled, trying to mask the relief she felt when the door slid open. She couldn't let the cameras catch that moment of weakness. Drones didn't feel anxiety. Drones didn't feel relief.

She stepped inside. The door slid shut behind her, but the tightness in her chest remained. The justicemen could be on their way. It wasn't uncommon for bad drones to be locked in their units before judgment came. Only the justicemen could free them, and "freedom" was just another word for punishment.

She shouldn't worry. Worry was dangerous. It only made her more unstable. But her mind raced. She didn't want to turn on the infoscreen, but it had to be done. Drones weren't allowed to sit in silence in their units. The screen had to be on, keeping them connected to the Monarch.

The static, filled voice of a smiling woman beamed from the screen. "The Monarch ensures contentment," she said. "The Monarch ensures order." The usual platitudes. The words washed over her as she moved to the bathroom. She carefully slid the foam tile in the ceiling and felt for the envelope hidden there. Her hand brushed against it, and she sighed in relief. She really had found a hiding place.

She carried the package to her desk. Privacy. It felt foreign, yet essential. Why had privacy never mattered before? She knew the answer before her brain completed the question. Deep down, she understood. Privacy mattered now because she had begun to question. She defied him. Writing was against his wishes. And she was hiding her discontent, hiding from the very entity that gave her life.

The infoscreen's voice droned on, "Good news for all respectable drones. The Monarch is initiating a new program that will increase your value. Drones over the age of 18, with child, bearing organs, are required to participate. The Life Meter results are finalizing, and once all eligible drones gestate this year, rationing will come to an end."

She recoiled. The thought of bearing a child for the Monarch sickened her. Conceiving without a marital partner, without even the illusion of choice. But the Monarch had deemed it necessary. Who was she to question his judgment?

She moved to the computer. Questions swirled in her mind, but she couldn't type them, not directly. Perhaps if she softened them, if she entered them carefully, the system wouldn't suspect her instability. Drones were encouraged to ask questions, after all.

Who am I?

The answer came instantly:

You are C, 14243.

What is my purpose?

To serve and adore the Monarch.

The answers should have brought her comfort. They always had before. But now, they felt hollow. She hesitated, then typed:

Where did the Monarch come from?

In the beginning, the world was void and without form. Then, the Monarch came and brought the world to life.

The same answer. The same words she had heard all her life. But she couldn't accept them now. She had asked these questions before. Hadn't she? When? Time felt strange, disjointed. Memories that should have been recent seemed impossibly distant.

She hesitated again, then typed:

What is Olias?

The answer blinked onto the screen:

Olias is a group of enemy agents who strive to overthrow the Monarch. Their purpose is chaos, slaughter, and destruction.

The same response. The same narrative. But it no longer made sense. If Olias wanted only chaos and destruction, why would they fight the Monarch? Couldn't the Monarch, with all his power, bring both peace and chaos? The answers were becoming less comforting, less believable. She glanced out the window at the mammoth wall that enclosed Atlis. Did the wall keep the world out... or keep them in.

Agents. Enemy agents who thought for themselves. It couldn't just be subhumans or monsters. The system said there were no drones beyond the boundary, but there had to be something, someone, on the other side.

She sat at her desk and wrote:

> "Today scared me. The janitors cleaned my unit and almost found my notes. If they had, I wouldn't be writing anymore. The justicemen would have already taken me. Monarch Representatives

frown upon written records unless they're requested by the Monarch."

She paused, considering the words, then continued:

"It's strange to write by hand. We're not taught handwriting at the Institute of Enlightenment. My mother taught me when I was small, before I entered the system. They say handwriting is flawed, that it leads to mistakes and misinterpretation. The Monarch says the only logic that matters is the logic of the moment. All other logic is obsolete."

Her thoughts wandered, and she wrote:

"Why aren't we allowed to clean our own living spaces? Wouldn't it be more efficient? The janitors come daily for minor cleanings, weekly for major ones. They clean everything while we're at work. But why? Wouldn't it be easier if drones maintained their own spaces?"

She thought about illness, about the way the system saw drones as flawed, fragile. Unlike the Monarch, drones couldn't simply be repaired. They had to heal. They were inefficient. Imperfect.

She felt a pang of guilt for her discontent. The Monarch provided. The Monarch knew best. But she couldn't shake the feeling that something was wrong. She had begun writing what shouldn't be written, feeling what shouldn't be felt.

She remembered the dandelion she had seen on the way home. A single yellow flower, pushing through the cracks of the concrete. Greenery was rare, nearly nonexistent. The world had been stripped bare by humans long ago. The Monarch allowed only minimal greenery, to protect what little was left.

She wrote:

"There's more beyond the wall. I know there is. I don't know what, but I can't stop wondering. I can't stop thinking. And that... that is dangerous."

CHAPTER 8

The underground car hummed softly, its smooth glide through the tunnels a stark contrast to the cacophony of life above. Once called subway systems, these transit lines were now reserved for the elite.

The drones who toiled in the colonies had no knowledge of these luxuries. Many had no idea there even was emperors. Emperors never shared such amenities. For drones, transport meant crowded freight carriers or miles of weary walking. The thought of Emperors mingling with chattel in the tunnels was laughable. At least, that's what he always heard.

He smirked to himself; the edges of his jackal mask caught the dim blue lights of the tunnel. The mask of Anubis. His father's choice. A symbol of the underworld, crafted with obsidian and gold filigree, its sharp angles mirrored the harsh hierarchy that ruled their lives. Fitting. This world was a vast underworld, with the drones shambling like the dead and the gods above endlessly quarrelsome and corrupt.

The car hissed to a halt, and Trajan stepped onto the platform, his boots echoing against the black marble. The Hall of Concord towered ahead, carved deep into the earth like a cathedral to power. Its spires of volcanic stone stretched upward, bathed in the artificial glow of chandelier light. Inside, the air was thick with incense and the faint tang of aged wine, a blend of decadence and oppression.

The hall swirled with motion. Emperors clad in robes of silk and brocade moved like predators in a cage, their masks glinting, lions, wolves, eagles, serpents, all symbols of their imagined majesty. The finest of the Monarch's politicians.

Monarch. The very word left a bad taste in his mouth. The Monarch wasn't an entity as much as an order. It stood for: *Mechanized Oversight Network for Axiomatic Regulated Control of the Hive.*

Drones scurried between them. They balanced trays of wine and delicate hors d'oeuvres, their eyes downcast. The masks, though meant for tradition and security, served another purpose: anonymity. Behind them, an emperor might hide his emotions, a bodyguard might impersonate a ruler, and suspicion could fester unchecked.

His gaze sharpened as he spotted the familiar gleam of ivory and gold. Tiberius and Nero stood near the hall's center, their masks reflecting their usual arrogance. Tiberius, with his wolfish grin barely hidden, and Nero, the lion, his predatory aura a constant reminder of his violent tendencies.

"Trajan," Tiberius greeted, his voice dripping with mock warmth. "What a delightful surprise."

Trajan stepped closer. His jackal mask was likewise meant to lend him an air of menace. "A gathering of legends, I see."

"Legends, indeed," Nero added, his tone sardonic. "Though I imagine Winter would have loved to be here."

The words struck like a blade. Trajan's hands tightened into fists beneath his cloak. "Winter understood her place," he replied evenly, though his voice carried an edge.

"Did she?" Nero tilted his head. The lion mask gleamed. "Attachment weakens us. You should have known better."

Trajan stepped closer and lowered his voice to a growl. "Some of us value more than mere survival."

Nero chuckled, low and menacing. "Survival is all that matters. Sentimentality gets you killed."

Tiberius placed a hand on Nero's shoulder, steering him away. "Let's not waste our breath, Nero. Some lessons are learned only through pain."

Trajan watched them disappear into the crowd. Their laughter lingered like acrid smoke. He turned toward a table and sank into a chair, his appetite gone. Around him, emperors murmured in hushed tones, their eyes flickered toward him, their masks hiding whatever venomous thoughts they harbored. He picked at his food absently and forced himself to maintain his composure.

A familiar voice cut through the tension. "Trajan."

He looked up to see Marcus, the only emperor he could stomach. His mask, a simple bronze falcon, was understated compared to the others' ostentation. "Marcus," Trajan said, his voice softening. "I didn't expect you."

He sat across from him as he glanced at the other emperors with distaste. "I debated coming. But here I am." He paused; his expression darkened. "I heard about Winter."

"Yes." Trajan's gaze drifted toward the trio, Tiberius, Nero, and Caligula. "One of them killed her."

Marcus nodded grimly. "That's why you never get attached to chattel. They sense it, Trajan. They exploit it."

"Come on, Marcus. Drones aren't chattel. They're people." He muttered and swirled the bourbon in his glass. "They had no right. No emperor is supposed to interfere with another's district."

"In a perfect world...." Marcus replied. A nearby drone stumbled under the weight of a tray. Nero struck the servant without hesitation. His laughter rang out. Marcus's lips tightened. "But this world is far from perfect."

Trajan leaned closer. He lowered his voice. "How do they get away with it? What gives them that kind of power?"

"Politics," Marcus said simply. "And because they crave cruelty. The system thrives on control. Drones must fear, emperors must strive, and those at the top must remind the rest of us who holds the leash."

Trajan's gaze hardened. "I don't want to live like this. My father reveled in this nightmare. I refuse."

Marcus sighed, finishing his drink. "Be careful, Trajan. They don't forgive rebellion. And they'll kill you if they think you're a threat."

Before he could respond, a sharp voice rang out through the hall.

"Emperor Trajan IV," the announcer called, his voice echoing ominously. "Please come to the stage."

The room fell silent. All eyes turned to him. His heart pounded, but he kept his chin high, his steps deliberate. He had seen dethronings before, public spectacles of humiliation and death. His breath tightened as he ascended the steps, but his mask remained firmly in place and shielded his apprehension.

He approached the stage, his thoughts racing. Whatever awaited him, he would not bow. These emperors believed themselves gods, but he knew the truth: they were parasites, feeding on the blood of the powerless. And one day, they would answer for their sins.

CHAPTER 9

She searched for the dandelion after work, but it was gone. Vanished, as if it had never existed. A strange emptiness filled her, a feeling that mirrored the grayness of the day. But every day in Atlis was gray. How had she never noticed?

It wasn't just the overcast skies. Everything was gray: the buildings, the roads, the paths. All of it was concrete or pavement, an unbroken landscape of gray stretching as far as the eye could see. There was something else, too, something deeper. She felt... sadness.

Her eyes stung, and she quickly looked down so the cameras wouldn't catch it. Tears? That was impossible. Drones didn't feel sorrow. They didn't cry. Emotions were inefficient. Drones who felt emotions were defective. Life was not sad. It wasn't happy. It just was. Sorrow was a biological impossibility for drones.

The earthmen must have eliminated the flower. Drones weren't allowed to encounter natural greenery, except what was carefully sanctioned within the division. Greenery contained allergens and toxins that made drones sick. It was too much of an expense for the Institute of Wellness to allow such risks.

She waited for the lift in the apartment building lobby, her mind drifting. History lessons flickered in her thoughts, vague recollections of humans who once lived in mountains and meadows. Where had that come from? Who had said that? It wasn't possible.

Humans couldn't have lived without the Monarch. Drones couldn't survive on their own, let alone in the wilderness. Life wasn't livable without the Monarch's protection. She loved and hated the entity that knew the past, the present, and the future.

History spoke of ancient races, ancient nations, long before the Monarch. They had survived... somehow. But drones couldn't survive beyond the borders of Atlis. How had those humans managed? She didn't fully doubt the Monarch, of course. Drones couldn't doubt the Monarch. But the questions... the questions wouldn't stop.

History said the earth had been decimated by 2000 BCE, but if that were true, how had humans survived long enough to populate the colonies? There wouldn't have been any life left. Maybe the Monarch really had preserved human cells, recreated the species in the Institute of Fertility. That was what they said, anyway.

She shook her head. She had to figure it out. But she couldn't ask anyone. Drones were required to report any behavior that could be considered remotely treasonous. There was no gray area. To ignore treason was to commit it. If she confided in anyone, both she and the person she told would be sent to the Institute of Clarity. But, it wasn't like she had friends of any note. Friendships were prohibited. The Monarch was the only friend all drones needed.

They were taught that enemies everywhere, countless agents envied the Monarch's perfection. It was common for parents to report their children for suspicion of treason. Parental units turned in one another. Even grandparents reported their families to the authorities. Treason was everywhere, always lurking just beneath the surface.

Now, she was outside that system. She wouldn't turn anyone in. She couldn't. She never had. She had no choice but to keep her thoughts to herself. That was the only way. She couldn't lie. She was discontented. Maybe even dangerous. It was only a matter of time before she became unhappy, even though that was also forbidden.

She stared out the window of the lift as it rose. She hadn't taken her vitamins. She hadn't taken them in a long time. All good drones take their vitamins. She'd heard that her entire life. The Monarch required it. Vitamins kept drones healthy, kept them from falling ill.

It was too late now. If she got sick, so be it. She didn't want to go to the Institute of Wellness. They would know she hadn't been taking them. They would see it as a refusal. And refusal was treason. But she hadn't refused. She had just forgotten. She knew in her heart it was moot.

Her thoughts circled back to the dandelion. Its elimination still gnawed at her. Anger, another forbidden emotion. The earthmen had destroyed it, of course, but why? It was just a tiny flower, too small to be a threat. The only thing in the city that hadn't been fashioned by the hands of men. She was fashioned by the Monarch, as were her neighbors. Everything in Atlis was created by the Monarch, for the Monarch.

She longed for something, anything, that hadn't been touched by his hand. But maybe she was too late. Maybe nothing existed anymore that wasn't Monarch, made. And maybe none of it mattered. Maybe she didn't matter.

It was only a matter of time before they found out. The Thought Monarch would soon be implemented, and when that happened, she would be discovered. She was doomed, and she knew it. Whether it was the fog, or death, it was coming for her. All she could do was make the most of the little time she had left.

CHAPTER 10

A stranger emerged from unit A, 8. She looked away the moment his gaze met hers. Drones didn't make eye contact, such behavior was inefficient. But a stranger was unusual. What had happened to C, 37237?

She listened quietly as the floor supervisor gave him the standard rules for the building. His name was K, 33528, but that would change soon. The Monarch always changed the designation to match the division. He would become C, 33528.

He must have come from far away. His appearance was different from the rest of the drones in the division, but that didn't matter. Noticing the appearance of others was forbidden. Physical attraction was inefficient, discriminatory, and unnecessary.

All drones were created equally, not for one another's pleasure, but for the glory of the Monarch. The Monarch didn't care what drones liked. Drones couldn't be trusted to know what they liked.

And yet, despite the Monarch's wisdom, she couldn't deny the pull of something unfamiliar. She smiled at him, just for a moment, and he smiled back. It was brief, but it was enough.

His eyes met hers in a way that no one else ever had. It wasn't the vacant gaze she'd grown accustomed to. He saw her. Her stomach tightened, and she quickly looked away, retreating into her unit as he did the same. The cameras were always watching, waiting.

How long had it been since she'd seen a new face? Ten years? Fifteen? Every day was the same: the same faces, the same routines. Once, that had been enough. She wished it still was. Life had been so simple before. No worries of being caught, no fear of discontent. She wasn't a saboteur then. Not like now. Now, she was an enemy agent without an agency behind her.

Life had become bizarre. The strangest things had gained importance, things that should have been insignificant. A dandelion. The sky. The feel of fabric against her skin. Privacy. None of it had mattered before.

Maybe it was best to delay reprogramming, even if the Monarch forbade it. She couldn't let go of this new world she had discovered. It was just as magical as it was terrifying. If she was eliminated for her disobedience, so be it. It was better to die with her feelings intact than to have them erased.

The janitors delivered her food supply for the week that evening, just as they always did. She stared at the packages on the table, guilt gnawed at her. The food came ready to eat, sealed in disposable containers. The Monarch had provided all of it. He gave her everything, and yet she doubted him.

She had heard rumors of a time when people purchased their own food, but that seemed absurd. Drones were incapable of handling such things. History stated that half of humanity had starved before they accepted the Monarch's wisdom. The Monarch promised the food was good for them, filled with the nutrients they needed. So far, it was.

Humans once cooked their food, too, or so the stories went. In kitchens... rooms dedicated to preparing meals. The thought was irresistible. It meant having control over what she ate, instead of consuming only what helped her contribute. But that wasn't her choice. Drones couldn't be trusted to make decisions about food.

She stared at the sterile white packaging. Each item bore the familiar green checkmark of approval. The symbol was everywhere in their lives.

Without thinking, she tore the labels from the containers and ripped them into tiny shreds. The act felt good for a moment, but guilt followed quickly. What was the point? She was an ingrate. She prayed the janitors wouldn't notice the missing labels.

Her grandmother had once whispered of a time when people were responsible for their own food. Despite her skepticism toward the Monarch, she found it hard to doubt her grandmother. That was a new and unsettling development. She had never placed anyone above the Monarch before. Now, she remembered her grandmother with such sentiment that she would sacrifice anything just to see her again.

Her grandmother had gone to the Institute of Longevity long ago, a reward for a lifetime of loyalty to the Monarch. The Institute was said to be a lavish resort for the aged, where they were cared for until the end. But she could never visit her. She could never see her again.

She realized, with a sinking feeling, how alone she was. The Monarch's company had always been enough. Until now. Until sentience. That's what it was, sentience. She had awakened, and everything was different now.

The clock on the wall startled her. It was time for the evening salute. She didn't want to go. Drones were required to gather in the street every night to salute the Monarch. Wrist scans served as both worship and surveillance. Those who didn't show were sent to the Institute of Clarity without question.

She gasped, she was already five minutes late. She bolted from her unit, running down the hall. Jogging was allowed indoors in emergencies, but she hadn't run in so long she couldn't remember. Fortunately, the scanning process usually took an hour. Stragglers weren't punished, but she didn't want to find out what happened to those who didn't show up at all.

She tripped coming out the front door, but no one noticed. She didn't believe any of the cameras captured it. Falls were serious. The floor supervisor would have to treat her injury if anyone saw. The cameras were pointed away. She was safe, for now. She glanced down at her leg, the fabric of her Monarch, approved leisure outfit had shifted, exposing a scraped shin. She quickly adjusted it, hiding the wound.

The representative scanned her wrist and moved on without a word. She didn't make eye contact. They would know if something was wrong. They would see it in her eyes. She briefly smiled at her neighbors, but they didn't look back. Something was wrong with them. They didn't look at anything at all.

She had never noticed it before. Their eyes were vacant, hollow. Before sentience, she had been like that, too, hadn't she?

Her thoughts were interrupted by the sound of footsteps. She could hear her own shoes hitting the pavement, followed by the synchronized rhythm of an entire block of drones. The sound was deafening. She had never heard it before.

She felt someone watching her. She didn't know how, but she felt it. That wasn't supposed to happen. Drones weren't supposed to *feel* things like that. Maybe she was becoming a freak of nature.

History said humans once had feelings, irrational, illogical emotions that made them weak, inferior.

She held her breath. She was caught. She knew it. They had seen her. The enemies of the Monarch were everywhere. Maybe they were waiting to abduct her, to take her beyond the boundaries.

She glanced around, trying to blend in with the other drones. Her heart pounded. She was about to sigh in relief when she saw him. The stranger from unit A, 8 watched her from across the street. Again, their eyes met.

He approached. Her pulse quickened, and for a moment, she feared it was heart failure. She couldn't run now. A public display of panic or illness was a one, way ticket to the Institute of Wellness.

"Hi," he said softly. His blue eyes remained on hers.

"Hi," she replied, unsure of what else to say. Words failed her. The moment felt heavy, wrong, and yet... she didn't want it to end. She didn't know what to do, how to react. Maybe the Monarch had made a mistake in placing him here.

They exchanged a few words about the evening, glancing around constantly, mimicking the other drones. Always watching for someone who might be watching them back. She sensed he was like her, waking up to something new, something dangerous.

The floor supervisor drifted closer, and they parted with a nod.

Back in her unit, her stomach fluttered with an unfamiliar feeling. Affection? For a neighbor? No one could ever know. Sentiment was a weakness, a vice. Sentiment meant something fallible had greater value than the Monarch. Sentiment was the first step toward treason. But it was a delicious feeling, and drone or not, she felt it for him.

CHAPTER 11

The hall fell silent as Trajan stepped toward the stage. His footsteps echoed like a drumbeat of judgment. Hundreds of masked faces turned to watch, their expressions hidden but their scrutiny palpable.

The air buzzed with expectation, thick and heavy under the chandelier light. Trajan adjusted his jackal mask. The cool metal pressed against his skin and grounded him. The familiar weight felt like a shield and a burden, a second face to conceal the roiling storm beneath.

At the podium stood Emperor Augustus II, his lion mask radiating authority with every movement. Augustus was a figure of legend, revered and feared in equal measure.

His division thrived with ruthless precision. Productivity soared under his reign, and his drones were the model of compliance. They called him the immortal emperor, a man who had outlasted rivals, scandals, and coups. He was the embodiment of the system's ideals, unyielding, efficient, untouchable.

"Trajan," Augustus said, his voice booming and resonant. He spread his arms in a grand, theatrical gesture. "Come forward. Tonight, we honor you. Your division has achieved population stability like no other. Tell us, Emperor Trajan, what wisdom can you share with your peers?"

Trajan's lips curled into a forced smile beneath his mask. He approached the podium slowly, his heartbeat loud in his ears. Taking the microphone, he hesitated. He weighed each word like a weapon that could misfire.

"Sure," he began, his voice steady but clipped. "The key is balance. Allow drones as much free time as work time."

The hall stirred. Muted whispers spread through the crowd like ripples across a still pond. Augustus cocked an eyebrow behind his mask, his interest piqued. "Free time?" he echoed, his tone laced with skepticism. "Doesn't that make them complacent? Lazy?"

"It doesn't seem to," Trajan replied, keeping his tone neutral. "As long as their medication supply remains uninterrupted, they remain compliant. The balance ensures they stay healthy and productive."

Augustus tilted his head, studying him. "And what do they do with all that free time? Doesn't it encourage them to think?"

Trajan met Augustus's gaze, even through the veil of their masks. "No," he said evenly. "The medication prevents overthinking. If anything, the rest makes their conditioning more effective."

A low murmur rippled through the audience again, tinged with faint amusement and curiosity. Augustus smiled, a predator's smile, honed by decades of survival. "You've given us much to consider," he said, nodding approvingly. "Is there anything else you'd like to share with us, Emperor Trajan?"

Trajan hesitated. His mind flashed with truths he would never utter. He wanted to tell them about the horrors beneath the surface, the degradation, the violence, and the endless cycle of cruelty. He wanted to call out the representatives who turned drones into disposable toys, the guards who used fear as sport. He wanted to rail against the blind indifference that ruled the lives of everyone in this hall. But he knew better.

None of them cared. None of them ever would. To speak out would mean death, not just for him, but for anyone who might still depend on him.

Instead, he let his shoulders relax, his tone flattening. "Just ensure your drones are healthy and well, cared, for," he said, the words barely audible. They sounded hollow, even to him.

Augustus inclined his head as though he had delivered profound wisdom. The crowd clapped politely. Their approval was as superficial as the glittering masks they wore. He returned the microphone and stepped down. He was ushered offstage with mechanical efficiency.

As he descended the steps, his stomach churned. His moment on the stage felt like a trap he'd narrowly avoided. For a brief, dizzying moment, he had expected them to denounce him, to strip him of his title, or worse. He had seen it happen before, an emperor torn apart for speaking out of turn, their legacy erased like an inconvenient stain. But no. His words had passed unnoticed, his message dismissed as banal advice.

As the applause waned and the murmurs of conversation resumed, he realized the truth. They didn't care. They never had. The lives of drones, the so, called backbone of the Colony Order, were nothing but numbers in a ledger. Replaceable. Disposable.

Beneath his mask, Trajan's jaw tightened. He scanned the crowd, their gilded faces blending into one monstrous, collective mask. He was surrounded by predators who fed off the suffering of the weak. Augustus's voice droned on in the background, praising the system, congratulating the assembly. Trajan barely heard him. His thoughts churned with the same question that had plagued him for years: Was he the last man among monsters... or were they men, and he the monster for caring?

The primitives came to mind, the so, called hillbillies beyond the borders of the divisions. The Colony Order painted them as savages; feral beings unfit for civilization. But he knew better. He had seen them years ago. They enjoyed lives without the suffocating order of the colonies. They were human, no different from him or the drones. Yet they were free. They lived outside the system's control, away from its poisons and lies.

At least, that's what he wanted to believe. Maybe their freedom was just another illusion, like so much else in this world.

CHAPTER 12

She looked out her window the next morning. The sun strained to break through the heavy clouds, a faint glow behind the overcast sky. She could almost see it, almost. How had she never noticed before? The world seemed different now, but she couldn't decide if it was the world that had changed, or if it was just her.

She wished the sky wasn't so gray. The ruins atop the tallest buildings still smoldered, not from fire, but from memory. The Monarch had them smoke eternally, a warning to drones about the fate of humanity when it ruled itself. Those ruins were a memorial, a message: humans destroyed everything they touched. They had forfeited their rights to the world long ago.

She stared through the window, unmoving. For a moment, she almost felt sunlight. Drones didn't feel sunlight. They worked. They followed routines, repeated the same cycle every day. Work. Sleep. Occasionally, they attended community events, but there was little else.

Community events were predictable, a concert, most likely. Monarch, approved artists playing Monarch, approved music. All music was selected for the drones' benefit. Anything chosen by the Monarch had to be good, so drones accepted it without question.

Only those deemed worthy by the Monarch could call themselves artists. The rest were sent back to labor. It was inefficient to pursue a path for which one lacked talent. The same applied to motion pictures. All art had a purpose, a moral, a function. Everything was created with order in mind.

A commotion in the hall broke her thoughts. She cracked the door open and peeked outside. A bereavement crew stood outside unit A, 6. They carried a body on a stretcher, draped in a white sheet. That had been C, 55395, her neighbor for years.

She hadn't known her well, but she always seemed kind. At least, she thought she had been. Maybe. She couldn't actually remember ever talking with her. It made no difference. Drones were prohibited from negative feelings towards one another. They were all equal in the eyes of the Monarch. To think otherwise was arrogance.

The crew spoke in hushed voices, but she heard them. Her neighbor had eliminated herself in her unit. Impossible. Drones couldn't eliminate themselves in their apartments. Drones eliminated themselves all the time, it was proof of human fallibility, but the only known way was to walk off a building. All windows drones might encounter were sealed shut for their safety.

She wanted to ask the crew how it was possible but knew she couldn't. Drones didn't ask questions. They didn't demand proof or rationale. They accepted anything they were told, eagerly, and without reservation.

She'd seen suicides before. Several others had walked off buildings, plummeting to their deaths in front of her, driven by guilt or instability. It never bothered her before. It was common among saboteurs who couldn't face capture. The Monarch never stopped them. There were always more resources for the obedient.

The crew removed her neighbor's possessions, speaking softly as they worked. All personal items were incinerated along with the body. It was less clutter for the landfills. Besides, it was wasteful to redistribute possessions. They would only serve as reminders of failed drones.

Her neighbor had shown signs of instability, they said. She'd tried to treat herself, a violation of the health guidelines. It was against the Monarch's command to attempt self, treatment. Civilized society depended on trust in the system. And she had been so close to being sent to the Institute of Longevity. How tragic.

She closed the door, her mind heavy with unease. Her neighbor's fate mirrored her own. She had been trying to fix herself too, without permission. That was treason. She knew it. It was probably too late now, even for the Institute of Clarity. She had gone too far. Her thoughts were too tangled in this new world of awareness. The Badlands would be her destination.

To be taken to the Badlands and eliminated, or to be taken to the Institute and returned to the fog, which was worse? She didn't want to return to the oblivion of obedience. The Monarch had always provided answers before. She never feared, never doubted.

Life had been so simple. Now, she couldn't even bring herself to seek help from the Monarch.

Maybe her fate would be like her neighbor's. Elimination. But how? She didn't know how drones ended their lives indoors. It seemed like it would take a tremendous amount of effort.

Most drones didn't need to eliminate themselves. When their time came, the Institute of Longevity took care of them. After years of luxury, the Monarch gently put the aged to sleep, preventing pain and unpleasant natural deaths.

She recalled fragments of history from school. Centuries ago, people believed in the afterlife. But the Monarch had eradicated those myths. Religion had been an obstacle to order, a cause of violence. Now, drones worshipped only the Monarch.

The Monarch knew all. The Monarch controlled all. Science, created by man, had given birth to the Monarch, and science was the only necessary force for worship. Drones knew this because the Monarch had told them so.

She sat at her window, staring out. The Monarch's image, the square, jawed face of a male drone, lined the buildings, always visible from the street. Occasionally, a drone would salute the image in passing. She had a sinking feeling that the faces were watching her. That they knew what she had been doing.

No one knew much about elimination, not even the Monarch. It had always been, and it always would be. Drones weren't supposed to ponder what came after, but she did.

The idea of humans being recycled didn't make sense. How could failing bodies turn into new ones? And why did death have to precede the process? Bodies decomposed, like all organic matter. How could they be reborn from decay?

The salute was starting, and she met up with K, 33525 as usual. She loved listening to him speak. His voice sounded different, clearer than those around her. His eyes were a piercing blue, and they actually focused on her when they talked. Together, they wandered through the drones, always mindful to avoid suspicion. His presence quieted the chaos in her mind.

Her neighbors spoke as she did, monotonous, flat. She had been born into Division 5, as her parents had, and their parents before them. Ten generations had lived and died in this division, repeating the same routines. She loved history, but it always seemed out of reach, like fragments of a dream she couldn't fully grasp.

She remembered visiting the Institute of Recollection once. The memories were foggy, as if they had been taken from her. She could recall the display celebrating the Monarch's invention of electricity. It had been a gift to humanity, though it quickly became a problem.

Another exhibit discussed the Monarch's creation of the "internet," a primitive form of communication that had evolved into their current technology. The Monarch had saved humanity, forcing them onto a path of order and productivity. As they re, entered the building, K, 33525 whispered, "They didn't used to do that."

She glanced at him, confused. He didn't elaborate. Too many others were around.

Things were never different. Or at least, that's what she had been told. Life had always been the same, hadn't it? Her childhood had been routine. Her parents had lived in their assigned units, just as she did now. Couples lived in "separate, but, near" apartments, preventing abuse and emotional attachments. No drone could love another drone more than the Monarch. It was forbidden.

Even reproduction was carefully regulated. Couples seeking to conceive a child had to receive permission from the Monarch. And only one child was permitted per parental unit, a policy that had existed for generations.

Couples deemed worthy of parentage went to the Institute of Fertility. Eggs were fertilized via laboratories and implanted in the mother, who would then live at the institute until birth.

Children were raised in the Institute of Early Life for the first 5 years. It ensured they were healthy, vaccinated, and implanted with their axioms before returning to society. It also ensured their parents resumed productivity as quickly as possible.

She would ask K, 33525 what he meant when she had the chance. The floor supervisor monitored all drone behavior for signs of instability. Justicemen dealt swiftly with any violators. Verbal outbursts, physical confrontations, both were strictly prohibited. Anyone who was caught breaking the rules was sent to the Institute of Justice, and most never returned.

She turned her attention back to the window, watching the world below. Maybe she was wrong for questioning the Monarch. Maybe it was only a matter of time before they came for her.

None of it really mattered, in any regard.

CHAPTER 13

Trajan woke to the bitter taste of stale bourbon on his tongue and the relentless pounding in his skull. His hangover felt like a familiar adversary, one he knew too well. The meetings usually stretched endlessly. Days blurred into nights until time felt meaningless. He hated them... his fellow emperors, the representatives, the entire damn charade. A litany of reasons churned in his mind, but none of them mattered. Whether he wanted to kill them all or himself, the result would be the same: nothing would change.

He pushed himself upright. His head spun. He struggled to the window. Below, the drones shuffled through their endless tasks like clockwork automata. Their faces were blank and eyes vacant. To the untrained observer, they might have seemed content. Their lives defined by mindless labor and artificial purpose. But he knew better. It was an illusion. The fallen angels proved it.

The angels, as Nero deemed them, were the outliers. Drones who had glimpsed the truth, recognized the futility of their existence, and chosen the only freedom left to them. His division boasted the lowest number of angels, but he couldn't claim it was due to compassion or clever governance. It was the meds, the careful balancing act of control. Still, he understood them. One day, maybe he'd join them. A single step off the roof and it would all be over.

A sharp knock on the door snapped him from his thoughts. The unwelcome noise cut through the fog in his mind like a blade. He frowned. No one knocked here. The drones weren't permitted near the emperors' quarters, and most didn't even know emperors existed. He rubbed his temple, grimacing, and went to the door.

Marcus stood on the threshold, pale and drawn, his hawk mask tucked under his arm. Trajan blinked in surprise. Marcus? Of all the emperors, Marcus was the only one he could tolerate. Still, it wasn't like him to show up unannounced and looking this shaken.

"Come in," Trajan said, as he stepped aside.

Marcus nodded stiffly, his movements jerky, and stepped into the room. "I didn't know where else to go," he muttered. His voice was barely audible.

"What's happened?" he asked. Curiosity sparked through the haze of his headache. Emperors didn't have emergencies. Their lives were meticulously orchestrated, insulated by layers of power and privilege.

Marcus sank onto the couch, his hands trembling slightly. "Tiberius was assassinated last night," he spoke in a voice that was low and unsteady.

He raised an eyebrow. He wasn't particularly upset by the news. The world could do with one less emperor. Tiberius was a snake, and he ran his division like a Roman bloodsport. Still, assassination wasn't something emperors usually dealt with. "Assassinated?" he echoed. He retrieved a bottle of bourbon and poured two glasses.

Marcus accepted the drink with a nod. His grip unsteady. "It gets worse," he continued. "Julian and Vespasian were found dead this morning."

Trajan stilled, the glass halfway to his lips. Now, that was interesting. Emperors didn't just die. They were too well, protected, their lives stretched unnaturally long by science and privilege. "Assassinated?" he asked, though his voice carried more intrigue than concern.

Marcus nodded grimly. "So it seems. I thought I should warn you... in case they come for you next."

Trajan smirked, though it didn't reach his eyes. "Grateful as always, Marcus. You're a good man."

Marcus sighed heavily, the lines of his face deepening. "No. Good men aren't emperors."

Trajan chuckled softly. He swirled his drink in the glass. "Then maybe we should leave," he said. The words slipped out before he could stop them.

Marcus's head snapped up. His eyes wide with disbelief. "Leave? Trajan, that's madness."

"Probably," Trajan admitted with a shrug. He offered a faint smile. "But tell me this isn't a mad world."

Silence hung between them like a storm cloud, heavy with unspoken truths. Trajan hadn't intended to say it, but the thought had been with him for years. It festered like an unhealed wound. Why not leave? What was left for him here? Death waited for him within the colony walls, whether from assassins, his peers, or the crushing weight of the system. Any relationship he tried to foster would end in death. Outside, at least, the rules might be different.

Marcus exhaled slowly. The tension in his shoulders eased. "You've had too much to drink," he muttered, and brushed off the comment. "This isn't something to joke about."

Trajan watched him. He noted how quickly Marcus dismissed the idea, how much fear it sparked. "Maybe...." He replied with a nonchalant wave. "Just a thought."

But it wasn't. The idea rooted itself deeper in Trajan's mind as Marcus stood to leave. The moment faded into quiet conversation. The primitives beyond the colony's borders, the so, called savages, couldn't be worse than the monsters who governed within it. The Colony Order called them uncivilized, dangerous, and less than human. But he had seen enough lies to doubt the truth of that claim.

The door shut behind Marcus. He leaned against the wall, his drink forgotten in his hand. He didn't know if freedom existed outside the colony, or anywhere on the planet, but it didn't matter. Even the faintest chance of it was better than the suffocation here. Maybe he was mad. Maybe he wasn't. Either way, death would find him eventually. He'd rather meet it on his own terms.

CHAPTER 14

Another stranger appeared on her floor. She couldn't shake the feeling that something was coming, that the influx of new faces wasn't just coincidence. The latest arrival was an older man, moving into unit A, 6 where C, 55395 had lived. There was something familiar about him, though she couldn't place where she'd seen him before.

He kept to himself, but she watched. He wasn't like the other drones. His demeanor reminded her of K, 33528. His gray eyes were alert, clear, not clouded by the fog that enveloped so many others. His name was C, 22935, and somehow, she felt a strange connection to these newcomers. They seemed different, more aware than the drones she'd lived among for years. Were drones elsewhere so different, or was it just her?

She had never given much thought to the occasional new faces that appeared in the division. It wasn't her place to wonder. That was Monarch business, not drone business. Still, it was refreshing, in a way, to see something new. Anything to break the monotony.

She walked to the bedroom, then into the bathroom. The routine of cleansing called to her. She undressed and entered the shower stall, the doors locking behind her with a familiar hiss. The locks were there to prevent moisture from escaping, mold and mildew were signs of inefficiency, and inefficiency was forbidden. The nozzles overhead sprang to life, spraying her with soapy water. Drones couldn't be trusted to clean themselves entirely. The Monarch had solved that problem long ago.

Upright, standing still, she let the nozzles do their work, scrubbing her body with an efficient spray. It was her responsibility to ensure that her hair and crevices were properly cleaned, but everything else was automated. Five minutes. That's all the time allowed. Anything longer was a waste of water, and waste was a crime.

Once, humans wasted millions of gallons of water daily, through their inefficient living. They were incapable of cleaning their own homes, their clothes, or even their dishes without massive waste. The Monarch had fixed that, too. Janitors now took care of everything, soiled clothing, linens, all handled and returned without question. It was better this way.

She lowered her arms, but still she wished for just a few more minutes under the spray. She raised her arms again as the hot air blew through the vents, drying her hair and skin. The bathroom was as gray as everything else, gray tiles, gray glass. The glass shower doors were thick and heavy. Why were they so heavy? Surely that was a waste of resources, too.

When the air stopped, the ultraviolet light blinked on overhead. It killed whatever germs might have survived the cleansing, though the light always gave her a headache. How had humans survived before the Monarch? How had they not exterminated themselves, living in filth and inefficiency?

She returned to the window, her gaze drawn to the street below. Night was falling, and she found herself noticing the colors in the clouds, muted, but beautiful. The streetlights flickered on, illuminating the empty roads until curfew at 9:00 p.m. The universal curfew ensured that all drones were safe in their units. No exceptions.

Her eyes shifted to the Monarch's face on the building across from her. Its square, rigid features stared down at the street, omnipresent, watching. Why were things the way they were? Why did she have to serve the Monarch? Why was everything timed, controlled, regulated? Even the act of cleansing was a reminder of her servitude.

The infoscreen in her unit blared behind her. It was an advertisement celebrating the glory of the Monarch. She glanced at the drones in the street below. They saluted without hesitation, their faces blank, their movements automatic. She froze. She hadn't saluted.

Drones were supposed to salute the Monarch's image, even in their units. If she'd been outside, she would have been noticed immediately, dragged off to the Institute of Clarity for failing to show the proper respect. Her heart pounded in her chest.

She couldn't do it. She couldn't bring herself to salute. If anyone had seen... but no, no one had seen. She was safe. For now.

She turned away from the window, her heart raced. She hated the Monarch. That's what it ultimately was. As much as she feared him, she despised him. But she feared life without him even more. The thought of freedom, of a world without the rigid order the Monarch provided, filled her with terror. What would life even mean without him? And yet, that same order suffocated her, controlled every aspect of her existence. She was trapped in a cycle of devotion and hatred, unable to break free.

She stared at the Monarch's image on the screen, the rigid face smiling down at her with cold indifference. Somewhere deep inside, a part of her longed to destroy it. But she knew better. There was no escape.

CHAPTER 15

The balcony called to him. It always did in moments like this, when the weight of it all crushed against his chest, when his thoughts churned like storm clouds and refused to settle. Trajan stood at the edge. He gripped the cold steel railing. His eyes fixed on the sprawling city below.

The drones moved in rhythmic patterns, their tiny figures like ants from this height. They carried, constructed, and obeyed with mechanical precision, each action part of a system that consumed them without question. Yet even here, among the endless ranks of the compliant, the angels existed.

He spotted one now. A single figure stepped away from the swarm, their path erratic and slow. He watched them enter the apartment building below. Several moments later, they emerged on the roof. They wandered toward the edge of the structure, where the towering drop, off met the sky.

No one stopped them. No one ever did. Guards watched from their posts, indifferent. Drones down below didn't notice. They were conditioned to ignore the deviation. The angel reached the edge, paused, and stared into the abyss.

And then they were gone.

He closed his eyes as the faint sound of impact drifted upward, muffled by the wind. The angel didn't scream, nor did drones who saw the carnage. Angels never screamed. It was almost as if they found peace in those final moments. A calm that eluded everyone still shackled to this place. He envied them.

"Another one?" a voice asked from behind him.

Trajan turned. His hand still gripped the railing. A drone attendant stood in the doorway, their pale uniform stark against the shadowed interior of his quarters. They kept their gaze low, as was customary.

"Yes," Trajan replied, his voice quiet.

The drone nodded and disappeared without another word. The justicemen gathered around the bloody angel below. They would report the incident. Not that it mattered. Reports on angels, or any drone for that matter, rarely went beyond basic record, keeping. The Colony Order saw them as acceptable losses, an inevitable byproduct of a system designed to crush and exploit.

He leaned forward. His hands tightened against the steel. What would it feel like, he wondered, to let go? To join the angels, to step into the void and find an end to the weight, the emptiness?

A knock at the door interrupted his thoughts. It wasn't the sharp, urgent knock of Marcus's earlier visit, but a softer, more hesitant sound.

"Come in," Trajan said without turning around.

The door creaked open, and a drone entered, a woman this time. She moved carefully, as if afraid to disturb him. "Your evening report, Emperor," she said, her voice low and deferential.

He waved her closer without looking. She approached, placing a slim tablet on the table behind him. Her presence lingered longer than expected, and he turned to meet her gaze.

"You've seen the angel?" he asked abruptly.

The drone stiffened. Her eyes darted to the floor. "Yes, Emperor," she said.

"What do you think of them?"

The question hung in the air like a knife. Drones weren't supposed to think, let alone share opinions with their rulers. But there was something in her posture, in the way her hands fidgeted with the hem of her uniform, that made Trajan press further.

"Speak," he commanded, his tone sharper.

She hesitated. Her lips parting as if the words fought to escape. "They're... brave," she said finally, her voice barely a whisper.

Trajan's eyebrows rose. He hadn't expected that answer. "Brave?"

"Yes," she said. She glanced up quickly and lowered her gaze again. "To step away. To stop pretending... to escape."

He stared at her. The weight of her words settled over him. *Brave.* Was that what it was? The angels didn't act out of desperation or fear, but courage?

"Thank you. You may go." his voice softer now. The drone quickly nodded and retreated; the door clicked shut behind her.

He turned back to the balcony. The city stretched before him, a labyrinth of gray and black, its lights flickered like dying embers. Below, another walker broke from the flow, their steps slow and deliberate. His heart pounded as he watched, the pull of the abyss growing stronger for him. Part of him wanted to save them, but another wanted to escape, too.

Something stopped him. Not fear. Not hesitation. It was her voice, the drone's quiet words echoed in his mind. *Brave.* Brave to step away. Brave to stop pretending. Brave to escape.

What if he didn't step off the edge? What if bravery meant something else entirely?

The angels found their freedom in death. But what if there was another way to defy the system, to stop pretending? His grip on the railing loosened as his thoughts shifted. A seed of something unfamiliar sprouted within him, not hope, exactly, but resolve.

He stepped back from the edge, his breath steadied. For the first time in years, his path seemed clear. The system would kill him, one way or another. But he wouldn't make it easy for them. He wouldn't walk quietly into the void.

He turned away from the city. His mind calculated. If the angels could reject the system through death, then he would reject it through rebellion. The drones needed a voice. The angels needed a leader. And the Colony Order needed to be reminded that even emperors could become Saboteurs.

CHAPTER 16

It was the eighth day of this strange new world, and nothing had improved. If anything, life had grown more unbearable. Questions gnawed at her. Doubts clawed at the edges of her mind. They pulled her deeper into a place she never wanted to go. Concerns arose that she hadn't even imagined before. Maybe it was age. She'd heard that strange thoughts often crept into a drone's mind around the third or fourth decade of life. Maybe that was all it was.

Maybe there was hope. Perhaps she wasn't truly discontented, just confused. She visited C, 22935, hoping for a distraction. It didn't work.

He was anxious. He spoke in a low voice, his eyes darted to the walls as if the world was listening, which it always was. His sister had lived there before, in the very unit where he now resided. But she hadn't eliminated herself. The words struck her like ice. It couldn't be true. That couldn't be possible.

Her first instinct was to report him. Years of conditioning made it automatic. Suspicion. Report. Erase. But she hesitated. She didn't want to. He hadn't done anything wrong, just spoken forbidden thoughts. But thoughts alone shouldn't be punished. If she reported him, it would draw attention to her, too. And she had her own forbidden thoughts to worry about.

Her thoughts had been so loud lately, so intrusive. She couldn't remember a time when her mind had been this noisy. Maybe she had never thought before at all.

To imply that the Monarch, the all, knowing, all, powerful entity, was anything less than benevolent was the ultimate heresy. Humans were cruel. Humans were flawed. Humans destroyed. The Monarch saved.

To question the Monarch was to invite danger. Open doubt meant a swift trip to the Badlands, without so much as a trial. The Court of Inquiry existed to prosecute criminals and enemies of the state, but crime was nearly nonexistent in the divisions. Still, the court remained, just in case.

She had committed heresy, silently, on paper. She had doubted the Monarch in her mind and heart. That alone was enough to warrant decimation. Defamation was treason. Treason meant chaos, slaughter, and destruction, the three evils. And if she was a heretic, if she truly questioned the Monarch, then she must want those things. But she didn't. She only wanted peace.

She was like the older drones who were eventually punished for their quiet rebellion, regardless of their intent. Maybe she was a cowardly saboteur. Perhaps, one day, she would walk off a building herself. She returned to her unit as quickly as she could.

She would give it another week. If he was caught, she would know what to expect. If she was caught, there would be no surprise. The microphones in every unit listened for discontent. The Monarch waited for a misstep. It always ensured total contentment. Even the shrubbery outside was wired with recording devices, to listen for malfunction. Malfunction was waste. Waste was eliminated.

Her eyes flicked to the packet of food on the table. Tonight, it would be fillet of barley. The Monarch's favorite. Every meal served to drones was chosen by the Monarch, paired with vitamins to keep them in good spirits. She hadn't taken her vitamins in days. That was probably the root of her problem. She was sick. The sickness could be cured with vitamins. But somehow, she wasn't sure if the sickness was worse than the fog.

She was supposed to have her annual physical two weeks ago. They had called to cancel the day before her appointment and promised to reschedule, but they never did. The Monarch had never let her run out of vitamins before. Was that the cause of her current state? Could this be the Monarch's fault?

Or was it too late for her now? Maybe she was dying, beyond even the Monarch's ability to save. And what if her failure to follow up on the appointment was seen as defiance? It probably would have been forgiven had she called them back immediately. But she didn't. She had let it slide, not out of forgetfulness, but out of defiance. She hadn't followed the rules.

She couldn't blame the Monarch entirely. And she couldn't go back to that foggy, forgetful world. She was in a new state now, awake, aware. She would rather die in this new state than return to the old.

A knock at the door jolted her from her thoughts. Her heart lurched. It's them. Justicemen, surely. Or worse, the Black Guard. Her hands shook as she crammed her papers into the drawer of her desk and edged toward the door. She had to answer. If a drone didn't answer the door, the floor supervisor would be called. They would assume illness, and then the Justicemen would come anyway, to escort her to the Institute of Health.

She took a deep breath and pushed the button to open the door.

CHAPTER 17

Trajan's wrist throbbed as he cradled it against his chest, the dull ache a reminder of what the doctor had removed. The axiom had been embedded there for as long as he could remember, a seamless part of him, like a name or a shadow. But now, without it, his body felt alien, untethered. The absence left more than physical pain; it left questions that clawed at his thoughts.

He moved through the Institute of Health's polished corridors, his reflection glinted off the pristine glass walls. The air smelled of antiseptic and flowers, artificially pleasant, like everything in the emperors' sector. Drones didn't have spaces like this. Their clinics were dim, their treatment perfunctory. Emperors, though, were afforded sterility, comfort, and luxury, even when their bodies betrayed them. *Not chattel*, he thought bitterly. *Something more. Or so they tell us.*

Outside, the city buzzed with activity. The streets teemed with drones. Their movements synchronized in eerie perfection. No hesitation. No deviation. The drugs kept them that way, docile, obedient, dead inside. He watched them from the raised walkway. His wrist bandaged tightly and still throbbing. They didn't notice him, as if he were another machine, part of the architecture that loomed over their existence.

The doctor's words played in his mind. *Strychnine.* A fail, safe. His axiom wasn't just an identifier, as he'd always believed. It could have killed him with a single command. His mind raced as to why his father implanted him with a drone's axiom? The question lingered. Its implications twisting like a knife in his gut.

Drones didn't know that the word "axiom" was actually an acronym. The Axiomatic eXistential Identification & Oversight Module kept them closer to the Monarch than they ever knew. It allowed the system to monitor everything about an individual drone. Now, he knew he'd been just as monitored. An emperor. It was unheard of.

He shook his head and kept walking. The revelations about the axiom weren't even the worst of it. The real horror lay in what it meant for Winter. For Autumn. For Summer. The women who had once made him feel human. Women he'd been told died of accidents, sudden illnesses, or unavoidable tragedies. Lies. All lies. He always suspected it, but he never had such proof before. His father killed Spring, he knew. And another equally masochistic emperor had triggered the others' axioms and released poison into their veins.

The realization burned. It explained everything. Their sudden disappearances, the hollow condolences from his peers, the emptiness that followed. The truth left him raw, gutted. They hadn't just taken his happiness, they had erased it, replaced it with manufactured explanations that absolved the system of blame.

"Bastards," he muttered under his breath. His voice trembled with rage.

He reached the park. The single oasis of green in the concrete maze of his division. It was reserved for emperors and dignitaries, but no one else was ever here. Emperors didn't linger in the open. They preferred the opulence of their private lounges and the safety of their mansions. He liked the solitude. It was one of the few places he could think.

The iron rocker creaked beneath him as he sat, his gaze fixed on the fountain at the park's center. The water flowed in elegant arcs, catching the sunlight, its rhythmic splashes masking the distant hum of the city. He had spent countless hours here, once with her. Now alone.

The pain in his wrist felt distant now, overshadowed by the storm in his mind. His father's tyranny had shaped everything in his life. The endless betrayals. The toxic power struggles. The lies disguised as laws. Even now, dead and gone, his father's influence lingered like a specter, a shadow Trajan couldn't shake.

Thanks, Dad. The thought dripped with venom. His father had been a tyrant in every sense. He ruled with cruelty and manipulation. He forced Trajan into his twisted games and coerced him to act against his own morals. The women his father paraded before him had been disposable, their sole purpose to serve and submit. Trajan had refused to participate whenever he could. He endured beatings for his defiance.

He had wanted something real. Someone intelligent, aware. Someone free. But freedom didn't exist here. Not for drones. Not for emperors. Not for anyone.

The fountain shimmered before him, its beauty mocking. He clenched his fists, and the bandage pulled tight over his wrist. *It has to end,* he thought. *The Order. The axiom. All of it.* He didn't know how, but the thought filled him with a quiet determination.

Drones weren't inherently lesser. He'd seen their potential. The spark buried beneath layers of drugs and conditioning. Free them from the chemicals, and they could think again. Dream again. Emperors, though... Trajan wasn't sure they deserved freedom. Most of his peers were no better than his father. Their humanity was twisted beyond recognition. As for the elites, the Monarch Representatives, they were a disease. Parasitic. Malignant.

His father had ruled with the embodiment of everything wrong with the system. His death had changed nothing. The cycle continued. Betrayal. Murder. Lies. He tried to survive it, but now survival wasn't enough.

His thoughts raced. He weaved plans half, formed and reckless. He needed allies, but whom could he trust? Marcus? The man had his doubts about the system, but doubt wasn't the same as rebellion. The drones? They outnumbered everyone else a thousand to one, but their conditioning kept them blind to their own oppression.

And yet, they had angels, drones who saw through the facade, who rejected the illusion even at the cost of their lives. What if he could show them another way? What if he could lead them not to death but to freedom?

The idea gripped him, as wild as it was dangerous. He didn't know if it was possible, but he knew one thing for certain: the Colony Order wouldn't last forever. Nothing ever did.

He stood. His resolve hardened. The fountain splashed behind him. Its sound faded as he walked back to his quarters. The system had taken everything from him. Now, he would take something from it.

CHAPTER 18

She locked the door behind K, 33528. Her thoughts were spinning. The world had become strange, and his questions about the sky only deepened her sense of unease. At first, they confused her. Who visits a neighbor to talk about the sky? But she knew what he meant... beneath the surface of his words. He'd noticed it, just as she had. He was awake, like her.

The sky. It was more beautiful than she ever remembered. It was never bright, never warm. The years of environmental collapse had seen to that. Sunlight barely penetrated the thick clouds that hung over Atlis like a shroud, if it could get through at all. But now, she noticed. The sky had been nothing more than a source of dim illumination before, no more special than a lamp. It certainly didn't warrant attention. After all, she was a drone, a worthless, incompetent laborer.

Heresy or not, she wished to be more than that. She wanted to be *someone*. She wanted to have value beyond productivity. That was probably treasonous, another forbidden thought, but she couldn't help it. It wasn't the first, and it wouldn't be the last. Now that she had her thoughts written down, now that she had chronicled her small, insignificant life, she couldn't ignore them anymore. She couldn't incinerate her words any more than she could eliminate them from her mind.

A flash of anger coursed through her. Why did life have to be about glorifying the Monarch? Why was everything for him? It seemed wrong, though she didn't know why.

The Monarch was at war, but no one ever spoke of it. There were no updates, no reports, no information at all. No mention of when it would end, if there had been casualties, or even where the war was being fought. There was no war within the borders of Atlis, so it had to be elsewhere.

And yet, her suspicion grew, slowly, quietly, that the Monarch wasn't truly benevolent. She had no proof, no reason to think it, but the idea was there. It gnawed at the edges of her mind. Did the Monarch care about drones at all? She couldn't stop the foreign thoughts that entered her head.

She was discontented. That was clear. She was unstable. She needed reprogramming. But the thought of it made her shudder. The image of the man in the wheelchair flashed through her mind, Eph. That wasn't benevolent. She didn't know what had happened to him, or where they'd taken him. He hadn't been at the street corner for days.

Chaos, slaughter, destruction.

She stared out the window again. Her eyes drawn to the concrete heads of the Monarch that lined the streets. The statues were supposed to make drones feel protected, to remind them of the Monarch's power and omnipotence. His face was everywhere, a symbol of strength, of safety.

But what if someone needed to be protected from the Monarch? She had never heard an answer to that question. One day, she would need protection. One day, the ever, present, ever, watching Monarch would not be her savior. He would be her destructor.

Her gaze dropped to her wrist. For the first time in her nearly three decades of life, she truly studied the axiom embedded there. How had she never thought about it before? That tiny device contained everything about her, her medical history, her identity, everything the Monarch deemed necessary.

Drones who couldn't work, who were broken physically or mentally, were taken to the Institute of Longevity. Everyone said how wonderful it was, how well they cared for the patients. But no one ever returned from the Institute.

No visitors were allowed inside, not even family. They said it was for health reasons. They said that the outside world was full of germs and bacteria that would infect the patients. They said that everyone who went to the Institute loved it so much they wouldn't want to leave, even if they recovered.

A smiling drone on the infoscreen echoed her thoughts: "We know it's all for the best, because the Monarch tells us so."

But she didn't believe it.

CHAPTER 19

She sat quietly in her cubicle, her heart pounded, a thin layer of sweat covered her skin. All around her, drones worked feverishly. They processed paperwork for Atlis, like obedient cogs in the machine. They were mad. All of them. It wasn't she who needed the Institute of Wellness, they did.

Outside, the storm raged. The wind howled against the building's walls, making them creak, and the sky lit up with the flicker of lightning. Thunder boomed, like the endless hum of the looms in the Institute of Textiles. The storm seemed ready to tear the roof off at any moment, but no one noticed. They were focusing on their tasks, heads down, papers shuffling, oblivious to the collapsing world outside.

She bit her tongue. Her hand gripping tightly beneath the desk to stop herself from reacting. She couldn't show fear. She couldn't show emotion. The cameras were always watching... waiting for the smallest deviation. The wind outside screamed against the windows, and the floor vibrated with the thunder. The others didn't flinch. They moved through document after document, blind to the chaos that threatened to consume them all.

Her task was simple yet crucial, sorting correspondence, filtering out suspicious packages before they reached the Monarch Representatives. Everything was scrutinized. Paper was rarely used, and that made it all the more suspicious. Sometimes, the Monarch deliberately sent inflammatory materials through the system, to test for quality... to test for loyalty. Missing it meant reprimand. Reprimand meant the Institute of Clarity.

She just couldn't focus. The storm outside mirrored the turmoil inside her. The thunder was too loud, the lightning too bright. Why did no one else feel it? How could they continue their work as if nothing was happening? She couldn't stop thinking about the stories, an entire building collapsed under the weight of a storm, thousands of drones eliminated in an instant. She didn't remember where she'd heard it, or when. But it lingered, half, formed, a memory shrouded in the fog.

The shift alarm finally sounded. She exhaled in relief as everyone rose in unison. Another shift done. Another mindless routine completed. She didn't want to go outside, not in the middle of a storm like this, but there was no choice. To stay would be conspicuous. She moved with the cluster of drones. She mimicked their expressionless faces, their robotic march into the torrent.

The rain drenched her almost instantly. It soaked through her clothing and chilled her to the bone. She couldn't remember ever feeling so cold. The earlier fear was now replaced by a shivering, physical discomfort. The storm rattled her nerves, but this cold was different. It was real, tangible.

The voice on the infoscreen reminded drones to go to the shower if wet, "Please allow the shower to dry your body so you don't become ill." She peeled off her wet clothing and stepped into the shower. The heat from the blowers rushed over her skin, and slowly, the feeling returned to her body.

Work had been unbearable before the storm, but now it was something worse. She hated the dullness of it all. She couldn't think of the right word: *boredom.* That's what it was. The word felt dangerous on her tongue, but it was the truth. She was bored. The Monarch forbade boredom. It was another step toward discontent. And discontent was treason.

Her instability wasn't getting better. With each passing day, she felt herself slipping further from the drone she had once been. Reprogramming was inevitable. She should turn herself in to the Institute of Clarity, let them reset her mind. A smart drone never resisted the Monarch's will.

But something inside her fought against it. She didn't want to go back. The old state, the fog, it was suffocating. She remembered it, like looking through frosted glass, the kind that decorated the Monarch's temple, with its ever, watchful profile etched into the panes. The symbol of security. The symbol of oppression.

The Monarch didn't feel like protection anymore. He felt like a predator. She felt his eyes on her, even now. He saw everything, every thought, every emotion. And one day, he would demand retribution.

The infoscreen was a constant reminder of her place. Her shin ached from the fall the previous day, but it was a dull, distant pain now. Outside, the rain was slowing to a steady drizzle, cleansing the streets. She noticed new announcements on the massive screen signs outside. A woman smiled. Her face stretched wide with unnatural joy. She grinned from the picture. The caption read, "I did my part and bred for the Monarch."

She cringed at the sight. The lie was so obvious, it hurt. A woman who had bred for the Monarch wouldn't be on a poster. She'd be locked away, hidden from view. Those tasked with breeding new drones were never seen again. She didn't know who the woman in the photo was, but the image filled her with a rage she couldn't suppress. The urge to destroy the sign, to set it on fire, burned inside her.

But what did it matter? If her notes were found, if her thoughts were uncovered, she'd be sent to the Badlands. *Defamation equaled decimation.* She'd heard it for years. *Silence was safety.* But silence wasn't possible anymore.

The sky darkened again. She moved to the window, her eyes drawn to the distant boundary wall. What lay beyond it? The Monarch said monsters roamed the Badlands. Drones were forbidden from ever touching nature. Nature was sacred. Humans had destroyed the world once, they wouldn't be allowed to do it again.

But she couldn't stop dreaming about it. She imagined touching real grass, feeling the earth beneath her feet. Not the sterile, genetically modified greenery that filled Atlis, but real, wild nature. It was forbidden, yes. But why? What was so dangerous about feeling something real?

Her thoughts were broken by the soft hum of the Floor Supervisor passing by her door for the evening salute. She stretched out her arm, allowing her axiom to be scanned, and then returned to her seat by the window. The clouds parted briefly, and for a moment, she saw a star. A single star, glimmered like a shard of glass in the night sky. She had never seen a star before. It was mesmerizing. It flickered in and out of view as the clouds shifted.

How long before the Monarch forced her back into the fog? How long before this clarity, this sharpness, was taken from her? The worst part was the secrecy. The need to hide everything she felt, everything she thought. If anyone suspected instability, they would report it. *Tittle tattle lost the battle.* It was drilled into them from birth.

Instability was dangerous. Special interests, hobbies, anything that took a drone's focus away from the Monarch was forbidden. Only social causes were acceptable, but she wouldn't know about that. Politics were for the Representatives, not drones. Drones weren't allowed to interfere. They weren't allowed to think.

Her thoughts drifting back to the star as she sighed. Maybe she needed a vacation. A visit to the Humanity Spa might help. But even that was a lie. The spa was just another simulation, a white room filled with artificial landscapes, projected images of a world that no longer existed. She wanted something real. She wanted to feel something real.

Her bare feet pressed against the cool tile, and she shivered. She wasn't supposed to notice the temperature, but she did. She wasn't supposed to feel the paper beneath her fingers, but she did. She remembered she hugged her parents before they went to the Institute of Longevity, but she couldn't remember the feel of their hands. Had she ever felt their skin?

Touch was forbidden. Prolonged contact was seen as uncivilized. But why? Why was human touch, the most natural of sensations, considered so dangerous?

Her thoughts were dangerous, too. She knew that. But the world of touch, the world of sensation, was too beautiful to ignore. How could it be wrong? How could oblivion be the answer?

CHAPTER 20

Trajan sat hunched over a stack of manuals and schematics. The lamplight casting harsh shadows across his face. The books, thick with technical jargon and diagrams, detailed the intricate workings of the Colony Order: power grids, communication hubs, and the security protocols governing the Black Guard. These were not materials meant for emperors, but he had access. Power granted privileges, and Trajan had learned long ago how to exploit them.

His eyes scanned the blueprints of Division T, the linchpin of the Colony Order's electrical and communication systems. If he wanted to break the system, Division T was the weak point. The problem? It lay under Nero's control, its infrastructure guarded and its conditions harsh.

The Representatives had chosen it deliberately. They trusted the brutal efficiency of Nero's division to protect their secrets. Getting there would be an ordeal, days by train, longer if he relied on more covert routes. But every flaw in the schematics told him one thing: it was possible.

He flipped another page. He traced his fingers over the printed pathways of cables and conduits. His mind raced with possibilities; the words blurred as ideas bloomed. A sandwich sat untouched beside him, the bread curling at the edges, forgotten in his obsession.

A sharp knock pulled him from his thoughts, and he jolted upright. He closed the manual and slid it under the others. "Come in," he called, keeping his voice steady.

The door opened, and Marcus stepped in. His gaze immediately fell to the cluttered desk. "Good Lord," he said, his brow furrowed. "What's all this?"

Trajan leaned back in his chair, feigning nonchalance. "Just brushing up on some old engineering," he said lightly. "Haven't looked at these since school. I've forgotten how much of our system worked."

"Schematics and blueprints?" Marcus stepped closer. His eyes narrowed. "Planning to build something?"

Trajan gave a faint laugh. He hoped it sounded genuine. "Well, if I'm going to refresh my knowledge, I might as well do it thoroughly."

Marcus's gaze lingered on the papers. Suspicion flickered in his eyes. "You're not planning something foolish, are you?"

"Foolish?" Trajan tilted his head, his expression carefully neutral. "What could an emperor possibly do that would be foolish?"

"Don't give me that." Marcus's voice dropped. His tone edged with warning. "You know exactly what I mean."

He sighed and sat the blueprints aside. "I'm curious... that's all. Understanding how things work, there's no harm in that."

Marcus studied him a moment longer before he exhaled. "I hope you're telling the truth. For your sake."

Trajan steered the conversation away. "So, what brings you here?"

Marcus hesitated. He glanced toward the door before he lowered his voice. "I heard something you'll want to know. The Monarch Representatives are planning to consolidate divisions."

Trajan frowned. "Consolidate?"

"They're shutting down several areas," Marcus said. "Drone numbers are dwindling. Consolidation will save resources. At least, that's their excuse."

"What about the breeding programs?"

Marcus scoffed. "You think those have been successful? Drones aren't reproducing fast enough, and the Representatives won't admit it. Consolidation is cheaper than fixing the problem."

He tapped his fingers on the desk, and feigned disinterest while his mind raced. Consolidation wasn't a cost, saving measure, it was a sign of decay. The system wasn't as unshakable as it appeared. "Which divisions?" he kept his tone casual.

"Nothing official yet... but Tiberius and Nero's names have come up. Their divisions have suffered the most loss of drones." Marcus paused. "If it happens, their positions will be dissolved."

"And the Monarch will eliminate them?"

Marcus admitted. "I wouldn't put it past them."

Trajan leaned back. His mind whirled. If Monarch Representatives would now purge emperors, it meant the hierarchy was weakening. Cracks were forming, and he knew cracks could become ruptures. "That's... interesting," he said, keeping his expression neutral.

Marcus studied him, his expression was unreadable. He leaned closer and lowered his voice to a near whisper. "Maybe you should do something foolish, Trajan."

The words hit like a thunderclap. Was Marcus testing him? He managed to keep his expression calm, though his heart pounded. "After all your warnings?" he said with a faint smile. "Now you're the one talking recklessly?"

Marcus's lips tightened. "Sorry. Reflex. But you've thought about it, haven't you?"

"Thought about what?"

"Escape. Rebellion. Anything but this." Marcus gestured vaguely at the room, at the colony beyond it.

Trajan hesitated. "If I have... it's just idle fantasy. You know as well as I do that nothing can change."

Marcus's voice dropped lower. "Not alone. But there are rumors. About the underground."

"The underground?" Trajan frowned. "That's a myth."

"No, it's real. Smugglers use it. Some drones too. It's dangerous, but it's a way out."

"Smugglers? We don't have any. What would emperors need smuggled?"

"Weapons. Illegal drugs. I've even heard the first Marcus Aurelius had a whole family out there."

That got him. Why did Marcus talk about a family? It couldn't be. Not in this place. He shook his head. "You realize this talk could get us both killed?"

Marcus nodded. "Do you ever feel like they're killing us anyway? Slowly, day by day?"

Trajan's hand tightened around the edge of the desk. He felt it too, the suffocating weight, the endless monotony, the quiet despair. "What are you suggesting?"

Marcus leaned in, his voice a whisper. "We leave. Tonight."

"Tonight?" Trajan blinked. "You're serious?"

Monarch

"I'm done waiting," Marcus said. "Something's coming. I can feel it. The Monarch is planning something worse than consolidation. If we don't leave now, we'll never get the chance."

Trajan's heart raced. Marcus's determination was startling, but the idea stirred something in him, something dangerous, something alive. "If you're serious..." he said slowly, "then so am I."

Marcus's face lit with a flicker of hope. "I'll make the arrangements. We should make our excuses for at least a week. Tell them you're going on vacation. Gathered what you need. Be ready at 10."

As the door shut behind Marcus, Trajan leaned back. He stared at the schematics. The underground. An escape route hidden beneath the colony. If it existed, it could be their salvation, or their doom. Either way, he couldn't ignore the truth. This life, gilded and polished, was still a cage. And for the first time, he saw a key.

CHAPTER 21

K, 33525 visited again that evening. She wasn't sure why she looked forward to it, but she did. His presence had become a strange comfort, something she couldn't reconcile with the rigid teachings of the Monarch, but it felt so natural. She had become too accustomed to his company.

What confused her even more was why the Floor Supervisor hadn't intervened. They allowed him to stay longer than the prescribed 15, minute visitation period, a minor inefficiency, but drones weren't allowed inefficiencies. Only the superiors could afford to be apathetic. Why was that?

She hated the way he made her feel, feelings that went against everything she'd been taught. Feelings were inefficient, unproductive, dangerous. Yet she couldn't help but feel drawn to him, even if it terrified her. She'd gone so far down this path, a path of rebellion. She was already an enemy of the Monarch, even if she didn't want to be. The Saboteur's path, and now she walked it. She knew she would be caught, and she imagined herself as the poster child for all that the Monarch sought to root out.

K, 33525 talked about things she didn't fully understand, but it fascinated her. His world seemed larger than hers, richer somehow, as though he had seen and understood things far beyond the borders of Division 5. Tonight, he came to ask if she would walk with him after the salute tomorrow. She hesitated but consented. There was a pull, an inexplicable need to be near him, even though it was dangerous.

He also frightened her. His words, his warnings. He leaned closely. He whispered that she should never look anyone in the eye for too long. She knew that rule, to mimic those around her, to blend in, but the urgency in his voice was unsettling. The first step to drawing negative attention was not hiding the instinct to look into someone's eyes. The cameras were always watching, always ready to catch a hint of deviation.

The Monarch should have no issue if they walked together. Drones were allowed to walk together, after all, provided they stayed within their division and observed proper behavior. But still, the fear lingered. It crept beneath the surface of every interaction.

As they spoke, she mentioned running out of vitamins. His reaction was immediate. He leaned closely. His breath was warm against her ear, he whispered, "You don't need them."

Her heart raced at his words and the sensations. She glanced around, panicked. Her eyes searching for the Floor Supervisor. She was still in her unit, oblivious. "Speaking like that will get you reprogrammed," she whispered back, barely audible.

"I've already been reprogrammed," he said. It was so nonchalant. His smile almost casual.

Her eyes widened. "What?" she breathed, disbelieving. Reprogramming was something distant. Something that happened to other drones who went too far. She had never met anyone who had gone through it. "No one comes back from that."

"I did," he said, his tone calm. "But they warned me, if I ever become a problem again... they'll eliminate me."

The word hung between them, cold and final. *Eliminated.* It was such an ugly word, such an ugly thought. The idea of him being taken, of his life being extinguished by the Monarch, was unbearable. She couldn't allow it. Not him. He was unique, different, everything she wasn't. The mere thought of losing him made her chest tighten with panic. She couldn't go back to life without him. The idea was a kind of death, and the fear gnawed at her.

In a hushed voice, he added, "It's ok. Don't think about it. It's just propaganda." She barely had time to process the word when the sound of a door opening in the hallway interrupted them. He glanced quickly around. "Life is different now, yes?"

"Oh, yes," she whispered, her voice trembling with the excitement of finally having someone who understood. "It's so different... so wonderful."

He smiled, but there was a shadow behind it. "I have something to show you tomorrow. But you must keep it private. Can you do that?"

"Yes," she promised without hesitation, though her heart pounded with anxiety.

The Floor Supervisor reminded him it was time to return to his unit, but he was already leaving. His departure left her in a whirlwind of confusion and questions. *Propaganda?* That was the word he'd said. She had never heard it before, at least not that she could remember. The thought of asking him about it tomorrow was tantalizing, but dangerous. Everything he said seemed to peel back another layer of her carefully constructed world and revealed the emptiness beneath.

She couldn't stand the new state of awareness, but she feared oblivion even more. She feared what would happen to her, but more than that, she feared for him. If they caught him, they would take him to the Badlands, and he would be eliminated.

It was inevitable, and the thought of it absolutely devastated her. Why? She hadn't known him long. She shouldn't care at all. But he didn't deserve elimination. He was something special, something pure, something the Monarch hadn't crushed. And she, she was just a drone. A flawed, fallible creature who had allowed herself to feel.

Her growing affection was like a disease. It spread through her mind. The Monarch was right to forbid sentiment between drones. It was dangerous, illogical. Her feelings for him made everything else seem pale and insignificant. She cursed herself for feeling so weak, for being so human. And yet, there was a spark of hope buried deep within the fear. Maybe he wanted to take her somewhere, somewhere far from the suffocating clutch of Atlis. The thought made her heart race.

But hope was a double, edged sword. The infoscreen blared again and interrupted her thoughts with a commercial break. A smiling woman appeared, her face beaming with manufactured joy. The caption below her read: "Wonderful advancements are underway. As a new rule, all female drones sent to the Institute of Clarity are required to carry a child to show their love for the Monarch. This will ensure total compliance with the Monarch's dominion and prove their loyalty to the power that knows all things past, all things present, and all things of the future."

She felt lightheaded. *Chaos, slaughter, and destruction.* The hateful mantra filled her mind. It circled like a vulture. Her life was chaos. Her world had been slaughtered. And her future? It was self, destruction.

The words of the advertisement echoed in her mind. *The power that knows all things past, all things present, and all things of the future.* If that were true, wouldn't she already be caught?

The idea of becoming a Breeder remained horrifying. Breeders never married, never formed partnerships. They existed only to create new drones for the Monarch. If she were sent to the Institute of Clarity, if she became a Breeder, it would mean the end of everything. She would never be with K, 33525. Never feel his presence. Never share another secret moment.

Her heart sank. The future she feared was closing in... suffocating her. She had defied the Monarch, and there would be no forgiveness. The only question was how long she had left before the inevitable reckoning.

CHAPTER 22

A sharp knock on her door jolted her out of bed, heart pounding. She hadn't even dressed yet, still in her sleeping shirt and underwear. Panic surged through her. Something was wrong. No one knocked before work, and visitation wasn't allowed until after hours, strictly in 15, minute increments. The urgency of the knock told her this was no routine visit.

She rushed to the door and slid it open, her breath catching when she saw K, 33525 standing in the hall. His face was tense, eyes wide with worry. He stepped inside quickly, whispering, "C, 22935 vanished during the night. Everyone, including the Monarch, is looking for him."

The words hit her like a punch to the gut. C, 22935, gone? How? Did Olias get him? Or had the Monarch taken him for something he'd said? Her mind raced, but nothing made sense. The units were supposed to be safe. The idea of someone disappearing from their very midst seemed impossible. Yet, it had happened.

The weight of it pressed down on her chest and tightened her breath. She didn't know C, 22935 well, but the news left her lost in worry. A strange, unfamiliar pain lodged deep within her chest, as though something precious had been ripped away.

Tears welled up, and before she knew it, she was crying. Actual, uncontrollable sobs. She couldn't recall the last time she cried. Had she ever cried? Not even when her parents were taken to the Institute.

Now, everything she had suppressed since her awakening burst forth in a flood of emotion. She felt raw and exposed, as though the walls she had carefully built were crumbling to dust.

K, 33525 seemed to know exactly what to do. He glanced quickly down the hall to ensure the Floor Supervisor hadn't noticed. He darted inside her unit, nearly carrying her. The door closed softly behind them.

He held his finger to his lips and signaled for her to remain silent while she struggled to regain composure. Her cheeks flushed with humiliation. She had lost control in front of K, 33525, of all people. It was too much. The sadness and embarrassment twisted together, a tangled knot in her chest. What kind of person was she to fall apart like this? And in front of him?

Without a word, he unplugged the microphone in the lamp by her bedside. Her breath caught in her throat. She'd never seen such an open act of defiance against the Monarch. It both alarmed and intrigued her. He was putting himself at risk for her, right here in her unit. She would be blamed if they were caught, but so would he. He was willing to risk everything, and for what? For her?

He handed her a tissue from the box on her desk. "Don't show emotion out there," he whispered gently. "Ever. They know how to spot it."

"I don't know what's happening to me," she choked out, her voice barely audible between sobs. He moved closer and, without hesitation, wrapped his arms around her. It wasn't a simple hug. It wasn't a handshake. He held her. She felt herself almost collapse into him. Her body trembled with the weight of emotions she didn't understand.

"What's wrong with me?" she whispered against his chest. Her voice quivered. "Am I dying?"

"No, no," he reassured her, a soft smile on his lips. "You're perfectly normal. You're coming out of the fog."

She barely heard the words over the pounding of her heart, over the sound of his heartbeat. She realized, in that moment, that she had never heard another heartbeat before. His warmth, the steady rhythm of his heart, it grounded her in ways she couldn't explain.

"This week has been the strangest..." she began, her voice faltered.

"And the most beautiful?" he finished for her. His soft laugh filled the room. She nodded, too overwhelmed to speak. It was true. It was a beautiful new world, terrifying and exhilarating all at once. He could have reported her for her outburst. He could have called the Floor Supervisor, and that would have been the end of it. But he hadn't.

"How do you know so much?" she whispered. She was still fearful someone might hear the forbidden intimacy of two voices in one room.

"The Monarch took my parents to the Institute of Clarity," he said quietly, his expression hardened. "I never saw them again. But I've found people like me along the way." His fingers curled around her own. She realized how comforting it was, how natural. She could stay like this forever, safe in this stolen moment, but she knew it couldn't last. They would have to separate soon, and the thought made her ache.

"My parents never did this," she admitted softly, her voice barely a breath. "They never... held my hand."

The Monarch had always forbidden such intimacy between parents and children. It was meant to foster independence, to avoid attachment, because a fearful drone was an inefficient one. But K's touch felt like something she had always needed. Something she had been starved for her entire life. It filled a void she hadn't known existed.

"How long has it been since you've taken your vitamins?" he asked, his voice low.

"Two weeks," she whispered.

He nodded as though he had expected her answer. "That's why everything feels so intense. Colors, sensations, everything is sharper. You're experiencing a shock to the senses. It's overwhelming at first, but it will settle. Things will make sense soon."

"But what happened to C, 22935?" she asked, forcing herself to pull away from the comfort of his arms. The embrace couldn't last forever.

"I was hoping you'd help me look for him." K said, his voice steady but laced with urgency.

The suggestion baffled her. Drones didn't look for people. The Monarch was the protector, the one who found the lost, not other drones. "The Monarch locates the lost," she mumbled, more to herself than him.

But K's eyes held hers, unwavering. "C, 22935 considered you a friend. That means you have a responsibility to find out what happened. We're in this together."

His words stirred something deep within her. A sense of duty, of connection, things she had never considered before. Friendship? Responsibility? These were concepts meant for the Monarch, not for other drones.

"He doesn't take vitamins, does he?" she asked suddenly, thinking of C, 22935's sharp, alert eyes.

"Hasn't in a long time," K replied, his voice soft. "That's why his eyes are so clear."

For the first time, she truly noticed the vibrancy of K's eyes, blue and bright, like a sky she had never seen. The realization sent a shiver down her spine. "It's a beautiful world," she whispered.

K smiled, but there was an edge to it. "I'll come tonight at midnight. We'll look for him. For now, just call me 'K,' and I'll call you 'C.' No numbers."

Her heart skipped a beat. The idea of being referred to without her number felt scandalous, intimate, almost shameful. She was just C. It made her feel vulnerable in a way she'd never imagined, yet it was exhilarating.

"Midnight is forbidden," she said, her voice trembled. She should stay in her unit. The idea of wandering at such a dangerous hour, alone with K, made her pulse quicken in both fear and excitement. This was madness.

"You let me worry about that." He stood and helped her to her feet. "Bring only what you can carry. A small satchel, some clothes, and anything you truly value."

"Mementos?" she asked, confused. Drones didn't have mementos. They weren't allowed. Sentiment was a weakness, a vice that had no place in the perfect world of the Monarch.

He smiled knowingly. "I'm sure you have a note, or something small, something personal."

Her eyes widened. How did he know about her writing? How could he possibly know? It was impossible, unless he understood her better than anyone ever had.

"When I turn the microphone back on, say something casual," K instructed as he moved toward the table. "Say, 'The janitor needs to service the lamp.'"

She didn't want him to turn it back on. She didn't want this moment to end. But she followed his direction. When he was satisfied, he cracked the door open, checked the hall camera, and darted back to his unit.

The room felt impossibly empty once he was gone. She looked down at her hand, still warm from his touch, and a strange unease settled over her. What was wrong with her? Why didn't she want to be alone?

She needed to prepare. The hours until midnight ticked by, and as she packed a few belongings into her satchel, she caught sight of herself in the tiny utility mirror. She froze, staring at the reflection of a woman she had never really noticed before. Pale skin, dark almond, shaped eyes, straight black hair. She didn't look like her parents. She didn't even look like herself. She looked... different.

She wasn't sure who she was anymore, but she knew one thing: tonight would change everything.

CHAPTER 23

Trajan finished his supper. The tasteless meal settled uneasily in his stomach as he sank into the plush chair across from the television. The evening stretched heavily around him. The sky outside deepened to indigo. Twilight's dim embrace felt like a weight on his shoulders, a reminder of the oppressive monotony of his life.

Marcus's visit lingered in his mind. For a moment, he'd dared to believe his old friend might actually act on his words. But no. Complaints were easy. Action? That was the province of fools and martyrs. He wasn't certain which category he fell into.

He absently rubbed his wrist. The dull ache from the missing axiom grounded him. Without the chip, he felt lighter, untethered from the colony's invisible leash. Yet the freedom felt hollow. What good was freedom if the system still wrapped its coils around his life?

The Monarch television droned in the background. Its endless cycle of propaganda was a mocking reminder of the colony's power. For the drones, contentment was pure compliance: glowing tributes to the Monarch, stories of miraculous progress, all punctuated with chirpy slogans. For emperors, the programming was equally insidious. Endless streams of pornography promised pleasure without consequence. The "celebrity" channels followed the Representatives, flaunting their extravagant lives, designed to inspire awe and envy. Both were distractions. Both were chains.

He flipped through the channels, his lip curled. The Representatives, the Monarch's pampered elites, paraded their wealth and power and smiled for cameras as if they weren't puppets on gilded strings. The porn was worse. A grotesque carnival of indulgence, carefully curated to keep emperors dulled and sated. He switched it off with a scoff.

The colony was built on addiction. The drones were drowned in drugs that stole their lives, and the emperors were fed endless temptations to keep ambitions dulled. Both groups were enslaved; they just wore different collars.

The knock startled him. Soft, hesitant, but unmistakable. He rose cautiously. His thoughts sharpening as he crossed the room. For a moment, he wondered if some assassin stood on the other side. Somone, likely from Nero. He opened the door and just found Marcus, cloaked in black, his eyes wide and burning with purpose.

"Marcus?" Trajan asked. He stepping aside to let him in. "Are you serious?"

Marcus nodded. His movements were quick and deliberate. "Dead serious."

"I didn't think you'd actually go through with it," Trajan closed the door behind them. "Emperors complain about the system every day, but that's all it ever is. Complaints."

"Not tonight." Marcus's voice carried an edge of desperation, but his posture exuded resolve. "Tonight, we do something."

Trajan studied him for a long moment, then nodded. "What's the plan?"

Marcus set a small, black security badge on the table. Its edges worn from use. "This. I lifted it from one of the techs. It'll get us into the tunnels."

"Tunnels?" Trajan frowned. "What tunnels?"

"The old subway lines..." Marcus lowered his voice. "Before the colony, the system was built on an underground network. Some of it still exists. It's how smugglers today move between divisions."

His pulse quickened. "Even if the tunnels are real, how do you plan to get through them? They'll be crawling with guards."

"Only a few," Marcus said, leaning forward and pointed to various spots on the open map. "Most of the system has been abandoned. The guards only patrol active entrances, but there are routes they don't know about. I've mapped one. It runs from here beneath Divisions S and U, straight to Division T."

"Division T?" Trajan's heart skipped. "The brain of the colony? Marcus, that place is a fortress. We'd never make it past the first checkpoint."

"We don't have to," Marcus countered, his voice sharp. "I've been studying. The main control node doesn't sit in the heavily guarded zone. It's in a maintenance sector, accessible... if we're smart."

He hesitated. The idea was madness. The Monarch's systems were vast, omnipresent, designed to crush rebellion before it began. Yet there was a gleam in Marcus's eyes. A wild hope that refused to dim. He found himself unwilling to extinguish it. To the contrary, he felt his own sense of hope grow.

"And when we get to this node? What then?" Trajan asked. "You think we can just... turn the colony off?"

"The Monarch is a machine." Marcus said simply. "Machines break. They malfunction."

He exhaled. His mind raced. How the hell did Marcus do it all before him? "If you're wrong, we're dead."

"If we stay, we're dead anyway." Marcus's voice softened. "You know that."

Trajan nodded slowly. "What do we tell the attendees? They'll notice we're gone."

Marcus smirked. "Tell them you're going to the spa. No one will question it. Emperors vanish for weeks all the time."

He almost laughed. The absurdity of it all felt surreal. He grabbed a small bag and began packing: a water flask, spare clothes, and a knife he wasn't supposed to own but had kept for years. He added a flashlight and a handful of energy bars.

"What about the axioms?" Trajan asked. He tested Marcus again. It just felt too good to be true. "If they track us...."

"They don't," Marcus interrupted. "At least, not emperors. The axioms are more about control than surveillance."

He bit back his reply. He hadn't told Marcus his chip was gone, hadn't shared how his own father had set him up for death. If this was a trap, that secret might save him. For now, he let Marcus believe he was still tethered.

They remained silent for a while after the exchange. The weight of what they planned pressed down on them. Trajan thought of the other emperors, Nero, Tiberius, the bloated ranks of the self, satisfied. None of them would even dream of doing what he and Marcus were about to attempt. They were lost in their vices, too blind to see the cage around them.

"Ready?" Marcus asked, his voice low.

He slung his bag over his shoulder, the weight familiar, almost comforting. "As ready as I'll ever be."

They slipped out into the night. The cool air bit at his skin. The city stretched before them. Its towering structures lit with cold, white light. The apartment windows were all black. The only light came from the streets below. Even in darkness, he felt the Colony's heartbeat pulse around him, relentless and suffocating.

"Even if we fail," Marcus said as they made their way toward the tunnels, "at least we'll fail trying."

He glanced at his friend and saw something he hadn't seen in years: hope. Not the shallow, fleeting hope of distractions, but a fierce, defiant hope that refused to die. For the first time in a long time, he felt a kinship with someone who appeared to feel what he felt.

CHAPTER 24

A gentle knock startled her awake at midnight. She fell asleep in the chair, waiting. She rushed to the door. Her pulse raced with the sudden urgency. If the Floor Supervisor caught them, it would be over. Everything would unravel.

It didn't matter that they were out searching for someone, rules were absolute. Drones weren't permitted outside after dark. And if the Justicemen found them? She had heard rumors of the punishment they called "full force," though she wasn't entirely sure what it entailed. All she knew was it wasn't something you came back from. Would they be facing weapons, traps, or worse, the mythical monsters of Olias that supposedly lurked beyond the city? The unknown gnawed at her.

K, 33525 stood at the door. His expression was serious but calm., He motioned her to follow without speaking. They moved quickly but quietly through the dark, empty hall. They traveled in the shadows. Every step felt like a potential disaster.

Cameras monitored the building day and night, but he knew their rhythm, their blind spots. They hugged walls and moved from her apartment door to the fire escape. The tiny red lights below the camera lenses were the only indicators of their position. Without them, they would have been completely exposed.

In the stairwell, he jiggled and yanked on a main wire that controlled the security feed. The red light flickered and went out. "That'll buy us time," he whispered. "They'll investigate eventually, but not before their shifts are over."

They descended the stairs in silence. Her footsteps were muted by the pounding heartbeat in her ears. They slipped out the back door and crouched behind a plastic shrub. Somewhere in the distance, footsteps approached. She held her breath. The footsteps paused, then moved away. Relief washed over her.

The outside world felt even more alien. At night, Atlis was a different place. The Monarch's strict rationing of electricity meant almost total darkness after ten o'clock. Every building was required to shut down all non, essential power. One lamp per apartment, heating, cooling, and the security systems, that was all. No streetlights, no city lights. The streets felt abandoned, lifeless. A few sparse lights dotted the sidewalks, creating faint pools of illumination, but most of the city lay in a blanket of darkness.

She had heard that humans in ancient times used open flames, candles, stoves, fireplaces, but the Monarch forbade such things long ago. Fire hazards, they said. Too dangerous for drones, who were inherently weak and incompetent. They could never be trusted with such things.

They made their way through the city. She grew more afraid as they moved deeper into unfamiliar territory. She had no idea where they were. Division 5's boundary was long behind them. She thought about celebrating the fact that she had crossed into foreign territory, but there was no time. They crawled under a platform as several Justicemen passed by overhead. The floor above them creaked with their heavy footsteps.

But these weren't the Justicemen she knew. They were Black Guard. They wore all black, their boots echoing ominously with each step. She could just make out the dark instruments strapped to their waists, tools or weapons, she couldn't tell.

They wore masks that completely concealed their faces, black eyecups hiding their eyes. The Monarch had always assured the public that weapons no longer existed in Atlis, except at the boundary walls. But from her vantage point beneath the platform, she doubted that promise.

K glanced at her and pressed a finger to his lips. The message was clear, stay silent. She nodded, steadied her breathing as they waited for the guards to pass.

The city felt more hostile at night than it ever had during the day. The silence was oppressive, broken only by the occasional sound of footsteps or the distant hum of machinery. They almost got caught twice, once they ducked into another bush, another time they hid behind a gate as patrols passed dangerously close.

After what felt like hours, they reached an old, crumbling building near the division's boundary walls. K led her inside through a side door, the hinges groaned as it opened. The interior was dark and damp, smelling of mold and decay. This wasn't part of Division 5 anymore. She wasn't even sure if they were in Division 7 or 8 at this point. She had lost all sense of direction.

"We need to remove your axiom," K whispered. He stopped her in a dimly lit room deep within the building. The ancient concrete walls seemed to close in on them, rusted steel beams exposed overhead like the bones of a long, dead beast. "We can't go beyond the boundary with it. The Monarch will trace you."

Part of her recoiled at the thought. Her axiom contained everything about her, her identity, her life. To remove it was to erase herself, wasn't it? Yet another part of her felt a strange, exhilarating relief. She couldn't go back now. There was no return to her unit, her job, or her previous life. A strange, hollow fear settled in her chest, but it wasn't sadness. It was something closer to anticipation.

They wandered through the maze of rooms until they found an odd man sitting beneath a bright lamp. His off, key singing echoed through the space, but he responded with surprising clarity when K spoke to him.

K handed her over to him. He introduced him as a doctor. The man worked quickly, injecting her wrist with something that numbed the area. K reassured her that the feeling would return soon enough. She felt nothing as the man expertly cut into her wrist and removed the tiny axiom and wrapped her hand with clean gauze afterward.

"I'll begin the transfer now..." the doctor muttered, as if to himself. He opened a nearby box and there was a computer in it.

"Transfer?" she asked, bewildered. He deftly connected the chip to the system.

K leaned in. "Your information is being moved to a secure system the Monarch can't access. It'll be sent to Fortune City."

"Fortune City?" The name sounded fantastical, like something from an ancient story.

"It's where we're going," He smiled, his voice soft. "I promised I'd take care of you."

She nodded, barely processing the information. It felt unreal, like a dream she couldn't wake from. Her mind spun, and her thoughts drifted to C, 22935. The mission to find him had seemed so important, but now, it felt distant, secondary.

Once the transfer was complete, the doctor crushed the axiom with a pair of pliers, shattering it into pieces. Just like that. She was free of all she ever knew as quickly as she might walk out of her building. "You don't need vitamins anymore, either," he added with a wry smile.

"They keep us healthy," she muttered out of reflex. Now the words rang hollow even to her.

"They keep you compliant," the doctor corrected. "Your vitamins are sedatives. That's why everything's been changing for you since you stopped taking them. You're waking up."

Waking up. The phrase hung in her mind. She was waking up, emerging from the fog. And yet, the world she was waking to seemed so terrifyingly vast. The doctor's words continued to echo as they left, his body soon just another shadow in the dark.

They fled down into an even deeper tunnel. They descended a circle in the ground. Her steps clanked on the metal ladder. The air grew colder and damper, and her footsteps echoed eerily in the underground passage. As they ran, the scream of a man reached them. "Oh my God!" His voice echoed in the distance, followed by hurried footsteps. K pulled her down a side corridor and turned off his flashlight.

"They got him," he whispered. "The doctor's dead."

She knew, deep down, they would be caught. She'd been foolish to think otherwise. The Monarch was everywhere. There was no escape. She pressed closer to K as they hid in the darkness. They listened to the sound of boots moving above them. The Justicemen, or worse, the Black Guard, had found the doctor. They heard the heavy thud of something falling down the ladder shaft.

K helped her back up the ladder after the sounds faded. They passed the body of the doctor. His lifeless eyes stared blankly at nothing. His body was unnaturally twisted. Blood leaked from his nose and ears. K's voice was flat, emotionless. "And this is what the Monarch really does."

As they moved deeper into the tunnels, her mind struggled to process everything. She wasn't just running from the city now, she was running from everything she had ever believed. The Monarch was supposed to protect, to guide, but now, she realized it controlled through fear.

They emerged into the open air beneath a vast, unfamiliar sky. Stars sparkled overhead, and the crescent moon hung low on the horizon. "Where are the clouds?" she whispered, confused.

"There aren't any here," K replied. "Atlis is under a dome. A screen."

The realization hit her like a wave. The sky above Atlis was a fabrication, a lie. Everything was a lie.

He led her through a ruined cityscape. Nature reclaimed what humanity had left behind. Grass and wild plants grew through the cracks in the asphalt, trees towered over broken buildings, and a stream of clear water babbled nearby. She knelt down, touching the grass with trembling hands. It was soft and real, more real than anything she had ever experienced in the sterilized confines of Atlis.

She soaked her feet in the stream. She felt the cool water wash over her skin. She knew she would never go back. This world, raw and untamed, was far better than the artificial existence she had left behind.

She was free.

CHAPTER 25

Trajan and Marcus stepped cautiously into the subway tunnel. Its gaping darkness swallowed the dim glow of the fading overhead lights. The air was damp and heavy. It reeked of rust and stale electricity. Their footsteps echoed faintly but were ultimately lost in the cavernous void.

Trajan gripped his pack tighter. His gaze darted to every shadow. "You're sure about this route?" he asked, his voice low.

Marcus nodded, a faint smirk on his lips. "It's not like we have a guidebook. But trust me, this gets us close."

The tension in his chest didn't ease. Every tunnel felt like a trap waiting to spring. The old subway lines hadn't been fully operational in decades, but they weren't abandoned. Smugglers used them. Black Guard patrols roamed them sporadically. And Marcus's plan? It relied on slipping past both unnoticed.

They boarded an ancient train. Its rusted exterior barely disguised the groaning machinery beneath. Marcus scanned their surroundings before muttering, "We'll switch direction at the next junction. Keeps us unpredictable."

He nodded and glanced over his shoulder. Each minute stretched interminably, every stop a new risk. The passing stations were a mix of desolation and decay, graffiti, covered walls, flickering neon signs advertising pleasures few could afford.

At one station, the remnants of a long, forgotten nightclub spilled out onto the platform. Emperors in gaudy robes stumbled about, their guards dragged along drones barely capable of walking. Trajan clenched his jaw. He forced his gaze forward. *Don't draw attention.* The station blurred into darkness as the train rattled onward.

Marcus leaned closer. "We're on schedule. A few more stops, and we'll hit Division M."

"And then?" Trajan asked, though he already knew.

Marcus's voice dropped. "Onto Division T. That's where the node is."

"Do you really think one node can dismantle the Monarch?"

"I don't think," Marcus replied. "I know. The code I have will unlock their central systems. Once it's in, the drones will wake up. No more compliance. No more lies."

"Who gave you this code, Marcus?" Trajan asked, his tone sharp.

Marcus's smirk faded. His expression hardened. "Tiberius gave it to Nero in case he was assassinated. I might've overheard...."

Trajan stared at him for a long moment, then nodded. Trust didn't come easily anymore, but Marcus was here, wasn't he? Whatever his motivations, they aligned, for now.

The train screeched to a halt in Division M. Its ancient brakes screamed against the rails. They disembarked into a world of chaos. The station teemed with life. Its underbelly exposed in all its grotesque glory.

Guardsmen staggered about, drunk on cheap liquor. Drones stumbled; their glassy eyes betrayed the numbing drugs that coursed through their veins. The sharp clang of combat drills echoed down the tunnel as a group of guards slashed at training dummies with unsettling fervor.

"This place is worse than I thought," Trajan muttered. He pulled his hood lower to avoid attention.

Marcus nodded grimly. "Stay in the shadows. We're just passing through."

They moved carefully along the edges of the station, avoiding the brighter areas where guards congregated. Music blared from a makeshift stage where barely clothed drones attempted to dance, their movements jerky and uncoordinated. The air stank of sweat, smoke, and spilled alcohol.

His heart pounded as they slipped past a group of guards who shouted obscenities at a female drone. One grabbed her arm roughly. He laughed as she stumbled. Trajan's hand twitched toward the knife in his pack, but Marcus's warning glance stopped him.

Not now, Marcus's eyes seemed to say. Focus.

They reached the far side of the station without incident. They slipped into another tunnel when no one was watching. Trajan exhaled slowly, his shoulders tense. "How much farther until we can rest?"

Marcus replied. "We'll rest soon. There's a place nearby."

The "hotel" Marcus had mentioned was little more than a glorified brothel tucked into the corner of an old station. The neon sign above its entrance buzzed faintly, some of the letters flickered out of sync. Inside, the air was thick with cheap perfume and despair. Drones shuffled about and offered their services in monotone voices. Their faces remained expressionless.

He grimaced as they checked into a room. The small, dingy space contained two narrow beds, a cracked mirror, and little else. He sat heavily on one of the beds, the springs creaking beneath him. The stale scent of unwashed sheets hit his nose.

"Wonder if they changed these," he muttered.

Marcus gave him a tired smile as he settled onto the other bed. "You're an emperor. You'll live."

They paused a moment and pulled their bedrolls from their packs. They spread them atop the covers. He laid back and stared at the cracked ceiling. Exhaustion pulled at him, but his mind refused to quiet. "You really think this will work?" he asked after a moment.

Marcus didn't answer immediately. "I don't know," he admitted. "But doing nothing isn't an option."

He turned his head and met Marcus's gaze. For the first time, he saw the desperation behind his friend's determination. Marcus wasn't just angry, he was broken. He seemed to cling to this plan as if it were the only thing keeping him alive. He could relate.

"Get some sleep," Marcus said softly. "Tomorrow, we move."

CHAPTER 26

She opened her eyes. She blinked against the unfamiliar dappled light that filtered through the branches above. For a brief moment, she was disoriented, unsure of where she was. Then it came rushing back, the escape, the new world.

Her tender wrist bled through the bandages during the night, but she didn't mind. It was her first night outside of a unit. Her first time sleeping on something that wasn't a sterile, impersonal platform. She was free.

Next to her, K slept soundly. His eyes were still closed. A peaceful expression softened his features. She didn't pull away. They had fallen asleep beneath a tall, overhanging tree, with cool earth beneath them, and open sky above.

She lay still. She was wholly content to watch the tree branches sway gently in the breeze. Everything here felt alive. No monitors, no screens, no watchful eyes hovering over her. There was no looming Monarch head to salute. No loud infoscreen blaring constant propaganda. She realized just how much she had grown to hate that continual intrusion.

For the first time in her life, she laid in the sunlight, unafraid. She enjoyed the warmth on her skin. There was no need to justify it as a waste of resources. It was heaven. K's eyes fluttered open, and when he smiled at her, her heart leapt in her chest. He wrapped his arms around her and pulled her close.

"This is either a hug or an embrace. It's okay to do the same." He murmured and pressed a gentle kiss to the crown of her head. She hesitated but then wrapped her arms around him in return, unsure of what to do but trusting the moment.

The sensation of human touch was still so foreign to her, yet K made it seem so natural. She had no experience with this, no one did... not in Atlis. His chin rested gently on her head as he softly spoke. "We don't use name codes out here. What do you want your name to be?"

Her name? She paused. Her mind went blank. "I can choose my own?" she asked, the concept foreign and strange.

"Yes," he said with a smile. "Out here, you're free to choose."

"But... drones can't name themselves," she murmured, her ingrained teachings surfacing. "They can't even name others."

"There's no Monarch out here," K reassured her. "We're not drones anymore. We're humans, and humans are capable of choosing their own names. Do you have one in mind?"

She stared up at the swaying branches again, thinking. A name. Something outside of the rigid identifier she'd been assigned. Something that was hers. It came to her like a whisper from a long, forgotten dream. "Selah," she said quietly. The name felt like it had always been with her, waiting to surface. She had imagined it before, perhaps in her room, maybe in a dream, but she couldn't remember.

"Selah," K repeated, smiling. "That's beautiful."

She smiled shyly. "Do you have a name?"

"I'm Ian," he said softly. "And C, 22935, his name is Vincent."

The sound of real names felt like a secret treasure. "This is heaven," she whispered, looking back at the sky. "I've dreamed of seeing nature for so long."

Ian kissed the top of her head again. "Yes, it is," he agreed, his voice warm. For the first time in weeks, her body, tense from the secrecy and terror of Atlis, began to relax. She felt safe. Weak and sore from the escape, she didn't want to move, but she knew they had to eventually.

They stood and ate a small breakfast of barley bars and carrot chips, the simple food tasting better out here in the wild. She splashed cool stream water on her face after eating and felt refreshed. Soon, they began their trek through the wilderness, meeting up with Vincent a few hours later.

"It's a whole new world out here." Vincent said as they trudged through the dense forest. "Use your new name as much as you can. It helps break the habit. It took me nearly a year to stop thinking in terms of identifiers. They train you well in the colonies. Drone indoctrination starts at birth."

Selah glanced back at Vincent, stepping over a fallen log as she processed his words. "Indoc... Indoctrination?" she repeated, unfamiliar with the term.

"Right. You probably haven't heard of that in Atlis. It's like brainwashing."

"Brainwashing?" The word conjured strange images in her mind, of someone scrubbing a brain with soap and water.

Vincent chuckled at her confusion. "Yeah, they must've rewritten the texts again. Brainwashing is when you convince someone of something false and get them to believe it completely. For example, do you remember who invented penicillin?"

"The Monarch," she said automatically.

"It was discovered by a man named Alexander Fleming," Vincent explained patiently. "Not the Monarch. And do you know who invented electricity?"

She frowned, feeling the conflict between her ingrained knowledge and the new information. "You know what I was taught."

"Here's a trick, no one invented electricity. It's a natural force. But Benjamin Franklin is famous for proving its connection to lightning. Thomas Edison, on the other hand, invented the lightbulb. Everything you've been taught about the Monarch inventing everything is part of the brainwashing."

They walked in silence for a while. Her thoughts continued to spin. So much of what she believed was a lie. She had always thought drones were numbered because they didn't deserve names. But now she knew. "Why do drones have codes?" she asked.

Vincent sighed. "One of the many methods of stripping away your humanity, to make you feel like a cog in the machine. If you're nothing but a number, you're expendable. Give someone a name, though, and they might start thinking they matter."

"What's out here?" she asked, glancing at Ian and Vincent. "Beyond the colonies, what kind of world is there?"

"A world free from the Monarch," Vincent said. "We're heading to a place called Fortune City. It's underground, mostly. The Monarch doesn't know the full extent of it, and that's how we survive."

The trees began to thin as they traveled farther and farther away. She saw the outline of buildings in the distance. "Are they really implementing the Thought Monarch today?" She asked as she slowed down as her feet grew heavy. Her legs ached.

"Yes," Vincent confirmed, his tone serious. "But it's a bluff or lie. Maybe they've figured out a way to scan emotions through the wrist axioms. But, regardless of what it can or can't do, it's still dangerous."

"And the breeding program?" Selah asked. A cold chill ran down her spine.

"They need more drones," Vincent said grimly. "That's what the Thought Monarch is really about finding out who's not compliant, rounding up the undesirables. I'm guessing all apprehended females will be forced into breeding as part of their reprogramming."

They crested a hill, and she saw the city before her. It wasn't like Atlis, no towering skyscrapers or sterile gray buildings. This place had charm and life. The buildings were smaller, worn but sturdy, and the streets were quiet. "This is Fortune City," Ian said. He guided her down the hill. "It's not much compared to what you're used to, but it's home."

They moved through the city streets, the buildings close and warm. People dressed in all manner of clothes, colorful and varied. It was like nothing she'd ever seen. "What are they wearing?" she whispered, awestruck by the diversity of fabric and style.

"Clothes." Ian replied with a smile. "Real clothes, not Monarch, issued uniforms. We'll get you some new ones soon."

As they entered a large building, she noticed the chandeliers hanging from the ceiling, sparkling in the light. Everything felt opulent, compared to the cold efficiency of Atlis. Inside, Ian led her to a small dining area, offering her a menu. She stared at it, overwhelmed. She could choose her own meal? That seemed impossible.

"I don't know what any of this is," she admitted, feeling foolish.

Ian smiled. "That's okay. I'll pick something for you." He ordered steak and baked potatoes, with sweet, iced tea. The meal, when it arrived, was unlike anything she'd ever eaten. The steak was rich and savory, the potato buttery and soft. It was overwhelming but incredible.

As they ate, Ian watched her, his eyes soft. "Are you happy?" he asked gently.

"Yes," she whispered, still trying to process everything. "I just... need to get used to it."

He smiled warmly. "You will. I'm here to help you."

Later, as they sat in the quiet of the room, Ian held her hand. For the first time since coming out of the fog, she felt like she belonged. This new world, with its dangers and uncertainties, was already more home than Atlis had ever been.

And she would never go back.

CHAPTER 27

It wasn't going to be as easy as he'd hoped. The gravity of his choice started to weigh on him. They'd traveled for what felt like days, and now they were on the way to board yet another subway system. Division Q was bleak, an industrial wasteland with little more than endless rows of warehouses and factories. Black smoke belched from every visible smokestack. It filled the air with the acrid stench of burning chemicals. *Thank you for keeping the environment clean, Monarch*, he thought with bitter sarcasm.

The irony gnawed at him, but didn't surprise him. The Monarch preached endlessly about protecting the environment, about safeguarding the earth from the destructive forces of humanity. But here they were, in a place that looked more like a war zone than a protectorate of nature. As was typical, the earth didn't need protection from humanity, it needed protection from the very system that claimed to be its savior. He shook his head but kept his thoughts to himself.

They found a place to camp for the night, atop one of the tall, abandoned buildings that loomed over the landscape like silent sentinels of despair. The building still had power, one of the few rare structures left without surveillance equipment, a small grace in an otherwise tightly controlled world.

Smoke continued puffed from hidden machinery rigged to appear as if some great battle had just taken place yesterday. Another twisted memorial to destruction. It was almost laughable. The Monarch itself was responsible for the very death and ruin these faux monuments claimed to honor.

After a careful exploration, they settled in. They plugged a small cooker into an old wall outlet and prepared a simple meal, their bodies grateful for the warmth. It was early evening, but both of them slept for that night and much of the next day. They were still on schedule. It was just safer to travel under the cover of darkness.

He had grown accustomed to the protective cloak of night, the way it wrapped him in a sense of anonymity and safety.

They poured over schematics and blueprints as they rested. Everything Marcus had painstakingly collected. The maps detailed routes through the city's substructure, forgotten and unused subway tunnels that hadn't seen activity in decades. They couldn't risk traveling publicly anymore. They were too far in, and the stakes were too high. Employees of the Institute of Technology, the Monarch's brain, were far too vigilant.

Planning their route through the tunnels shaved off a significant amount of walking time. It gave him a glimmer of hope. Maybe they really could make a difference. Maybe they could strike a blow against the Monarch's seemingly invincible system. The thought buoyed him, even though he knew how slim their chances were.

But they weren't alone in the darkness.

He was surprised at just how many others they encountered as they moved through the shadows. The majority were also slipping through the night like ghosts. In even heavily patrolled divisions, with rigid rules and watchful guards, the nights were teeming with unauthorized activity. He couldn't count how many others he saw, moving in and out of the shadows. They weren't drones, too aware, too alive. They certainly weren't guardsmen, either. So who were they? What did that leave?

The system was binary, you were either part of it, or you weren't. There was no in, between, no gray area for those who didn't fit. Yet here they were, people moving beneath the surface, unseen, unnoticed, part of some hidden underworld he'd only vaguely suspected existed. The Monarch loved to speak of Saboteurs, weaving stories of mythical rebels as cautionary tales, but he had always assumed they were just that, myths, used to keep the drones compliant. No one actually wanted to escape the colony, he'd thought.

But these people? Maybe they did. Maybe, like him, they wanted out. His heart lifted at the thought. They weren't alone.

At one point, they stopped to clear away grass and moss from an old sewer grate. The metal cover screeched as they slid it aside, revealing a narrow tunnel entrance below. Once inside, Marcus replaced the grate, their exit hidden again. The tunnels were long abandoned, the air thick with dust and decay. As they moved deeper into the labyrinth, he couldn't help but ask, "Do you really think they had a valid code, Marcus? We're pinning a lot on the words of two very unreliable emperors."

He hesitated for a moment, glancing over his shoulder as they walked. "You still nervous about that?"

"I'm asking, aren't I?"

Marcus said, his voice low. "I overheard them talking at the last meeting. They thought they were alone."

He mulled over the information. "Why would they care? They love the system." Nero and Caligula were the epitome of pro, Monarch emperors, hedonistic, cruel, and deeply entrenched in the power structure. They had more consorts and concubines than he could count and indulged in every vice the Monarch encouraged.

Marcus gave a dry laugh. "They've passed the point of caring about the system that sustains them. They want to raise hell and watch it all burn. They want to be the Monarch, themselves, and the only way possible is to destroy what exists. Remember the real Nero in ancient Rome? He supposedly said, 'I would that the world should burn before I die.' These guys are no different."

The pieces slowly fell into place. "My father was like that," he admitted, his voice soft. "He didn't care about the system either, just about having more of everything, faster. As I got older, he became more violent, more insatiable."

"The emperors who abused me were the same," Marcus said, his voice darkening. "I think the system deliberately turns emperors into monsters. It's easier to control someone who's so consumed by their vices that they can't think straight. And some of them go beyond that. They lose whatever soul they had."

They pushed open another rusty door and stepped out into yet another forgotten subway tunnel. This crumbling one was long abandoned. Only one bench remained intact, the rest had disintegrated with time and neglect. They sat and rested for a moment. The weight of their journey pressed down on them.

He thought of the path they were on, the dangerous game they played. It was all so fragile, one wrong move, one misstep, and they would be caught. But for the first time in years, he felt like he was fighting for something real, something that mattered. Maybe Marcus was right. Maybe they could bring the colony to its knees.

As the darkness enveloped them, he allowed himself a brief moment of hope

CHAPTER 28

They offered her an evening of movies, but she declined. Even if they weren't Monarch films, she didn't care to see another screen anytime soon. Ian seemed the most concerned about her. He sat next to her in silence, which she appreciated. There was too much to process, so many truths that had been lies, so many beliefs shattered. She was exhausting.

This must be what normal felt like, clear, headed, without the fog of the Monarch's drugs. Ian left to get them a snack. He returned with two steaming cups of hot chocolate. She stared at the cup, watching the liquid swirl and cool. Chocolate was forbidden in Atlis. It was deemed toxic. She tentatively sipped the drink, surprised by the rich flavor. Poison? she thought bitterly. It tastes like heaven.

A soft voice interrupted her thoughts. "Selah?" Ian said gently, "This is my cousin, Rose."

She greeted Rose, who extended her hand for a shake. The warmth of Rose's hand surprised her, softer than Ian's, almost delicate. Rose had Ian's same sharp features, but her presence was calm and reassuring.

"Hi, Selah. Welcome to Fortune City," Rose said warmly.

"Thank you," Selah replied, her voice still uncertain.

Ian excused himself. He went to find Vincent and ensure Selah's data transfer had been completed. As he left, Rose sat down beside her. "You're still in shock, aren't you?" Rose asked gently.

"I guess," Selah admitted. "I don't know what to do."

Rose smiled knowingly. "I felt the same way when I got here. It took months for the fog to fully lift. Ian and I both went through it. They took our parents when we were young."

"Did you go to the Monarch League?" Selah asked. The Monarch League was a place where orphans or children of 'Saboteurs' were raised. She knew it as a cold, distant place.

"Yes," Rose nodded. "We both did. That's where we decided to become cousins."

"Why did they take your parents?" Selah asked.

"They said they were Saboteurs," Rose explained. "We didn't understand it at the time, but we knew something was wrong. As soon as our vitamins ran out, we started waking up. Ian and I snuck out of Atlis together."

Selah's heart tightened. "How long did it take you to adjust?" she asked.

"Months," Rose said. "Maybe six or eight. I felt like I'd never stabilize, but it gets easier."

"Have many drones escaped recently?" Selah asked, realizing she wasn't alone in her awakening.

"Vincent's brought six in the last two weeks. Ian brought you."

"Just me?" She hadn't realized how special her escape was.

"Yes," Rose smiled. "Ian usually helps Vincent, but he went back just for you."

"Why?" she asked, surprised by the sudden connection. "Why me?"

Rose chuckled softly. "He's very smitten with you."

"He said I was special, but I didn't think, "

"He doesn't take things lightly," Rose cut her off. "He noticed you coming out of the fog. He was worried for you."

She felt a mix of emotions... gratitude, confusion, and warmth. She hadn't realized how deeply Ian cared for her until now. "I'm glad he did," she whispered. "I'd still be there if not for him."

"I'm glad you're safe." Rose replied.

They spent the evening talking about life in Fortune City. How to adjust, and the changes she would experience. It was almost surreal to watch the sunset outside the large windows. No more hiding her thoughts or her writing. No more fear of surveillance. She was free.

"What happens if we get sick here?" Selah asked.

"You see a doctor," Rose replied simply. "There's a clinic right across the road."

"And... vitamins?" Selah asked.

"You don't need them unless you want them, but that's not common," Rose explained.

Rose led her through the building to arrange sleeping quarters. The rooms were set up for new arrivals, people just like her, who had to adjust to a world without the Monarch. They were set up to look much like the apartments in Atlis.

It wasn't long before Ian returned. He confirmed that her information had been successfully transferred. Rose chuckled as Selah mentioned wanting to share a room with Ian.

"That means something different here," Rose said, laughing gently.

"But... we slept together last night," Selah replied, confused.

"It's a bit more intimate than that in Fortune City," Rose explained. "You need to get comfortable with yourself first. You don't have the Monarch to tell you how to feel or what to do now. This is your time to figure out who you are."

"Can Ian still visit me?" She asked and felt a bit lost.

"Of course. You don't need permission for anything here," Rose said with a smile. "Visits aren't timed like in Atlis."

As they arrived at room #17, she marveled at the size of the bed. It was large, soft, and inviting, nothing like the cramped sleeping platform she'd grown up with. A tiled bathroom was attached, with a stack of fluffy towels by a sink that Rose called a "vanity." A massive mirror hung on the wall.

"I've never seen a mirror that big," Selah admitted.

"You'll get used to it," Rose said. "You'll learn to dress how you want, look how you want. We'll go over cosmetics later."

"Cosmetics?" Selah asked.

"Powders, creams, things that make you feel beautiful," Rose explained.

"That's so... frivolous," Selah said, remembering how such things were condemned in Atlis.

"Very," Rose agreed with a grin. "But you'll find it fun."

She tried to rest after Rose left. She lay on the bed. She stretched her arms and legs out across the vast mattress. There was space, more space than she'd ever had in her life. The soft bedding enveloped her, and for the first time, she felt safe.

Her thoughts drifted to her parents. She seldom thought of them, but now, in this strange new world, she wondered what they would have chosen if they had been given the option. They loved the Monarch more than anything, more than her, more than each other. How could they have lived under such a system and still adored it?

A soft knock at the door pulled her from her thoughts. Ian stood in the doorway and held a small bunch of daisies. He entered and sat beside her on the bed. The flowers rested between them.

"I brought you something," he said with a warm smile.

She smiled. She took the flowers and inhaled their fresh scent. It was such a small thing, yet it felt monumental in this new life. Ian talked for a while about what to expect, what she needed to adjust to, but she couldn't focus on his words. Her mind was still turning with the enormity of everything.

Then, without warning, he leaned down and kissed her softly. Her breath caught in her throat. The simple touch sent a surge of warmth through her body. Something she had never experienced before. His lips lingered for a moment before he pulled back. He left her heart racing.

Her world felt suddenly brighter, more vivid. She hadn't wanted him to stop, but she was too shy to admit it. Ian seemed to sense her hesitation and smiled, understanding her confusion.

"Vincent will take us to see the boundaries of Atlis tomorrow," he said softly.

"Do I have to?" she whispered. The thought of returning to anything near the Monarch unsettling her.

"It's a necessary part of understanding what you've left behind. We'll be far from the actual boundaries," he reassured her.

She felt a weight lift as he spoke. For the first time, she was beginning to grasp the idea that her life was hers to control. No more codes, no more cold directives. She was free, and she could choose her path. But what path was that? She didn't know.

Her mind quieted as Ian began to care for her wrist. He removed the bloodied bandages, cleaned the wound, and applied fresh gauze with a tenderness that made her heart ache. She barely heard his words about the chip and its effects. Her thoughts drifted as she leaned into the warmth of his presence.

For the first time, she felt like she belonged, like she was more than just a number. And as Ian held her hand, she allowed herself to believe that maybe, just maybe, this new world was where she was meant to be.

CHAPTER 29

Someone had removed her clothes during the night. She awoke feeling disoriented. The faint warmth of morning sunlight streaming in through the window. For a brief moment, she panicked, unsure of where she was. Then, memories of the last few days rushed back, and she relaxed. *Fortune City.* She was in Fortune City, no longer in the clutches of the Monarch.

She realized she was dressed only in her undergarments. Her clothing had been neatly draped across a chair by the bed. Her shoes and socks placed neatly on the floor. The linens beneath her were soft, far softer than anything she had ever felt in Atlis.

She stretched out and then curled into a fetal position. She let the warmth of the bedding envelop her. She could stay here forever, hidden away from the world, free of fear and pressure. But a knock at the door shattered the tranquility.

Reluctantly, she slipped her Monarch, issued cotton shirt over her head and padded to the door. She cracked it open cautiously and found Rose standing there, dressed in denim pants and a pink cotton blouse. She held a plastic bag in one hand and smiled warmly.

"Ian sent this over." Rose said, as she stepped inside. "He wasn't sure if you'd want him to see you undressed."

"Why would that matter?" Selah asked, genuinely confused.

Rose chuckled softly. "Some girls don't want men to see them when they start to become aware of their bodies."

"Really?" She still didn't fully grasp the concept. Drones were never encouraged to think of their bodies as anything but functional.

"You will, too, eventually. Drones are conditioned to believe they have no gender, that it doesn't matter. But deep down, the Monarch hasn't fully erased that part of us."

"They tried?" Selah asked. She was intrigued by the possibility.

"Oh, yes," Rose said, settling into the chair by the table. "They tried everything, surgery, genetic experiments, you name it. They even tried to create asexual drones, but it never worked. Sentiment and attraction are too deeply ingrained in us. So instead of trying to physically remove gender, they rely on chemicals, sedatives, and constant anti, gender propaganda."

"Why did they keep gender at all?" Selah remained puzzled.

"Breeding," Rose answered matter, of, factly. "They can't replicate the womb. They need women to produce new drones. And they need men's... seed."

"Seed?" Selah giggled, as she pictured men sprouting plants from their skin. "Fruit or vegetable?"

Rose burst into laughter. Her amusement so genuine that tears formed in her eyes. She felt self, conscious, but Rose's laughter was infectious. She squeaked and wheezed, and that made the entire situation absurdly funny.

"You'll learn soon enough," Rose said as she wiped her eyes. "It's a long explanation, but not something you need to rush into."

Rose handed her the bag, and Selah pulled out the new clothing. It was beautiful, so different from the dull, utilitarian garb she'd worn her whole life. Rose called the fabric of the pants "khaki," and the white blouse was soft, with delicate lace and ruffles at the sleeves. She had never owned anything so pretty.

In Atlis, clothing was purely functional, designed for practicality. The undergarments Rose gave her were called a bra and panties, far more intricate than the simple, uncomfortable briefs and control, top tanks she'd always known. Rose even had to show her how to fasten the bra properly. It was all so foreign.

Once dressed, she stood in front of the mirror, awkwardly looking at her reflection. She had never really studied her appearance before. Drones weren't meant to care about such things. She felt strange, unsure of how to perceive herself now that she was out.

"You look much better," Rose said, smiling.

"I'm still in shock," Selah admitted, her voice low. The unfamiliar sensation of soft, fitted clothing against her skin felt both exhilarating and disorienting.

"It's okay. You'll be in shock a while," Rose reassured her. "Whenever you're ready, we'll help you find some cosmetics. There's no rush."

"Won't these clothes get ruined if we go outside?" Selah asked, still worried about practical matters.

Rose shook her head. "No, your pants are durable. Khaki is strong and stain resistant. The shirt's a cotton, canvas blend, also sturdy. I helped Ian pick out clothes that could handle the outdoors."

She ran a brush through her hair and glanced back at the mirror. It was strange seeing herself like this, but she liked it. She couldn't help but think how quickly the authorities in Atlis would drag her off to the Badlands just for owning such luxurious clothing. The bitterness she held toward the Monarch was still there, but now it was tempered with pity for the drones she'd left behind.

"They didn't choose that life," she muttered softly, more to herself than to Rose. "None of them did."

"No," Rose said. She overheard her. "They didn't. Just like you didn't choose it. But you were lucky. You escaped."

She stepped outside. The heat of the sun warmed her face. A line of four, wheeled vehicles idled in the street, engines rumbling quietly. Ian stood nearby and straddled one of the machines. He had an extra white helmet tucked under his arm. Vincent pulled up in front of her on another vehicle, offering her a smile.

"These are ATVs," Ian explained. "We figured you'd prefer these for your first ride. Motorcycles take a bit of practice."

Selah nodded, though she had no idea what a motorcycle was. She climbed onto the back of the ATV and wrapped her arms around Ian's waist. The day was already hot, the sun blazed overhead. Despite her nerves, there was a sense of adventure in the air, something new and exhilarating about traveling in the open wilderness. She never thought it existed, but here it was.

They sped across the countryside and the world blurred by in a rush of green and blue. She clung to Ian as they crested a hill. Her stomach flipped and tickled. She giggled despite herself.

"You felt it, too, huh?" Ian's voice crackled through her helmet.

"Yes! What was that?"

"G, force," he explained, laughing. "I'll take you out for fun sometime."

They rode in silence for a while. The landscape passed in waves of beauty. She marveled at the sheer openness of it all. She had never traveled so fast or so far in her life. In Atlis, drones walked everywhere. There were no vehicles. Even if there were, they had no reason to leave their divisions.

Her stomach tightened as they neared the boundary of Atlis. She wasn't ready to face the oppressive walls again. The looming threat of the Monarch. But now, she felt different. She wasn't a prisoner of that life anymore.

"Why do they applaud when someone makes it to the city?" She asked as the ATV bounced over uneven terrain.

"Because it's a miracle," Ian replied. "So many don't make it. Getting out of Atlis is almost impossible."

"Why do you keep going back?" she asked. "Why not just stay away?"

"You'll understand in time. Drones are slaves, mentally, emotionally, and physically. They don't even know they're enslaved. That's why we keep going back. To help those who can't help themselves."

The weight of his words settled over her like a heavy blanket. She remembered the fog of the Monarch, how it dulled her thoughts, kept her compliant. Had Ian not found her, she would still be there, sleepwalking through her life.

Her heart ached as she thought of the drones still trapped inside Atlis. They didn't know any better. They had no idea what freedom felt like.

CHAPTER: 30

Alarms screamed through the tunnels as Trajan and Marcus sprinted down the dimly lit corridors. The cold, metallic air stung his lungs. Behind them, the rhythmic pounding of boots echoed louder, closer, an unrelenting reminder of the Black Guard's pursuit.

"Faster!" Trajan barked. His voice hoarse from exertion.

"I'm trying!" Marcus shot back. He clutched his side and struggled to keep up.

The tunnel forked ahead. It split into three shadowy paths. Trajan grabbed Marcus's arm and yanked him toward the leftmost passage. Its narrower walls cloaked in dripping vines and grime.

"This way!" Trajan hissed. His voice was barely audible over the din of their pursuers.

They plunged into the tight passage. The faint glow of the overhead lights flickered ominously. The pounding of boots faded slightly, but it didn't stop. The guards were relentless, their pursuit guided by something more than guesswork.

"It's like they know where we're going," Trajan's mind raced as they pressed deeper into the labyrinthine tunnels. His eyes flicked to Marcus. "How?"

"I don't—" Marcus started, then stopped, his face blanching as realization struck. "Oh, no. No."

"What?" Trajan demanded, spinning on him.

"The axioms," Marcus whispered and clutched his wrist instinctively. "They must've flagged us when we entered Division R. We're being tracked."

He cursed under his breath. His mind scrambled for a solution. "We need to get it out. Now."

"There's no time!" Marcus protested, panic flashing in his eyes.

"They'll kill us if we don't," Trajan snapped, his voice cutting through the rising hysteria. "Do you have a knife?"

Marcus hesitated, then fumbled at his belt, pulling out a small, serrated blade. Trajan grabbed it without hesitation, motioning for Marcus to lean against the wall.

"This is going to hurt," Trajan warned, his tone grim.

Marcus nodded, his jaw tightening. "Just do it."

Trajan worked quickly. He sliced into the flesh of Marcus's wrist. Blood oozed down his arm and slicked the knife's hilt as Marcus clenched his teeth to stifle a scream. The axiom, a dull gray sliver, emerged from the torn skin, its edges glinting faintly in the dim light.

Trajan held it up. His eyes narrowed. "This little bastard's leading them right to us."

"What about you?" Marcus gasped. He cradled his wounded arm.

Trajan's gaze flicked to a nearby grate. A narrow sewer tunnel gaped below. Water rushed through it in a steady stream. He dropped the axiom into the current, and watched it disappear into the depths.

"Let's hope they follow it." He said and helped Marcus to his feet.

"What about you?" Marcus asked.

He held up his own wrist. His bandage was now dirty from their travel.

"What's that?"

"They removed my axiom the other day."

"What? Why?"

"Father dearest gave me a drone chip."

"Wow. He was a bastard."

"Yea, the poison was leaking and making me sick. They were supposed to replace it with a proper axiom sometime next week."

The sound of pursuing guards fading as they pressed on. They put more distance between themselves and the abandoned axiom. His heart still pounded in his chest.

He cast a sidelong glance at Marcus. He was now pale but still seemed determined. They wrapped his arm in a makeshift bandage torn from his shirt.

"Why didn't you think of the axiom sooner?" Trajan asked. His voice laced with frustration.

Marcus shook his head weakly. "I didn't think they could use it like this. Emperors aren't supposed to be tracked, at least, that's what we've always been told."

"And you believed that?"

"I didn't have a choice," Marcus muttered. "None of us did."

He gritted his teeth. The Monarch's lies infected everything. They twisted even the smallest truths into tools of control.

The tunnel sloped upward ahead. The air grew warmer and staler. They emerged into a massive drainage chamber. Its walls were slick with moss and filth. Rusted pipes crisscrossed above them and dripped foul, smelling water into the pool below.

"Where now?" Marcus asked, his voice ragged.

Trajan scanned the room. His eyes caught a faint red glow from a maintenance hatch near the far wall. "Up there," he pointed.

They scrambled toward the hatch. The distant sound of boots haunted their every step. Trajan wrenched the door open. It revealed another tunnel. This one was smaller, its walls lined with cables and flickering lights.

They moved deeper into the new tunnel. His mind churned with doubt. Something was wrong. The guards pursued them too quickly, too precisely. And then there was Marcus's axiom. He couldn't shake the feeling that something else was going on.

"How did they flag your chip, Marcus?" Trajan asked in a low voice.

"I don't know..." Marcus replied, his tone defensive. "I told you, I wasn't expecting this."

CHAPTER 31

A decrepit platform emerged from the shadows like the forgotten bones of a long, dead beast. Dripping water echoed softly from somewhere. A mocking metronome against the suffocating silence. The air was thick and stale, as though it hadn't been disturbed in decades.

They stopped. Their breath ragged after hours of navigating the labyrinthine tunnels. Trajan set his pack down and stretched. His entire being was nothing more than pain.

Marcus dropped onto a broken bench. His face pale. His hands trembled slightly. The portable lantern cast long, flickering shadows, and made the decay around them seem alive.

"I don't know how much farther we can go without rest." Trajan wiped sweat from his brow.

Marcus shook his head. "We can't stop too long. They'll catch up." His voice carried a quiet urgency. His gaze darted to the shadows beyond the platform.

Trajan crouched near the remnants of a fire pit, brushing aside ash and debris. "If they even know where we are," he said. The doubt in his voice betrayed his words. "It feels like they're following us."

Marcus didn't answer. Instead, he stared at the faint glow of their lantern, his jaw tightening. "They shouldn't be able to track us."

He sat slumped against the wall and cradled his bandaged wrist. "They'll think we're doubling back," he murmured. "It'll buy us time."

Their respite was brief. The distant echo of boots pounding on stone shattered the fragile silence. Trajan's head snapped toward the sound. His heart leapt into his throat. The Black Guard had found their trail.

"Time's up," he said. He pulled Marcus to his feet. "Let's go."

He stumbled but managed to steady himself. They grabbed their packs and darted into the nearest tunnel. The lantern swung wildly in Trajan's hand as they ran. The pounding of boots grew louder, accompanied by the sharp bark of commands.

"This way!" Marcus gasped. He yanked Trajan toward a narrow passage. The walls closed in and forced them to move single file. The air grew colder, and the ground beneath their feet turned slick with moisture.

"Where does this lead?" Trajan asked, his voice tight.

"Out of the grid," Marcus replied. "It's old, off the main system. They won't expect it."

He didn't trust Marcus's knowledge, but he had no choice. The tunnel twisted and turned. Each step pulled them deeper into the maze. The sound of pursuit ebbed and flowed behind them. The guards' voices were distorted by the tunnel's acoustics.

They burst into a wide chamber. Its ceiling was high and arched. Massive pipes lined the walls. They dripped water onto moss, covered floor. The air felt heavy here, oppressive.

"We need to block the path," Trajan said, scanning the room. His eyes landed on a rusted valve wheel near one of the pipes. "There. Help me."

Together, they turned the wheel, their muscles strained as it groaned in protest. Water gushed from the pipe. It flooded the chamber's entrance and created a slick, treacherous barrier.

"That'll slow them down." Marcus said as he panted.

"For now." Trajan replied. His eyes narrowed. "But they'll find another way. We have to keep moving."

The air grew colder and the lights dimmer, but they pushed further into the tunnels. He felt the walls close in. The oppressive weight of the Colony Order pressed down on them even here. The deeper they went, the more he wondered if they were truly escaping, or if the system simply toyed with them.

He couldn't shake the feeling that the Monarch itself was watching. Its unseen eyes tracked their every move. The system wasn't just a machine, it was a predator, and they were its prey.

But they wouldn't stop. Not now. Not while there was still a chance to fight back.

CHAPTER 32

After another hour, they reached the mountaintop. The air seemed to thin, and the world spread out below like a forgotten memory. Her legs and backside ached from the long ride. She winced as she rubbed her sore muscles. "Does it always hurt this much to come out of the fog?"

Ian dismounted from the ATV with a sympathetic look. "Usually."

"Why?"

"Remember when I told you your senses get sharper once you're out of the fog?"

She nodded.

"Well, pain gets sharper too. Everything feels more intense when you've been numb for so long. I'll get you some medicine when we get back."

Vincent handed her a pair of binoculars. "Here," he said, "look." He explained how they worked. She raised them to her eyes. She could peer over the top of the fortifications of Atlis.

Giant domes were positioned above Atlis in most areas. They kept the climate controlled below. This prevented sunshine from entering when the Monarch wanted. The domes were turned off on overcast days to save energy, and she was in luck. The day was overcast, for real.

She was shocked by what she saw. Inside the colony, where she had spent her whole life, the landscape was barren and unkempt. Nothing like the engineered greenery she once knew.

Red clay patches covered the ground. Dark stains littered everywhere, and nothing seemed to grow. A high, grimy wall surrounded this forsaken area, giving it an even more grotesque appearance.

"What is that? What Division?" she asked, her stomach twisting at the sight.

Vincent's voice was tight and filled with restrained anger. "That's part of Division T. The operating division of Atlis." He pointed to the drones that moved in a line. "Those drones are going to the Institute of Longevity."

She peered through the binoculars again. Her gaze fell on the drones, but they were escorted by Black Guard officers. Why? The Black Guard had nothing to do with the institute.

The figures moved through a lush garden, past a pristine pool surrounded by flowers. The sight seemed oddly beautiful, until her focus shifted to the group. They were a mix of elderly, a few children, and two adolescents, all smiled.

"What are they doing?" Her voice cracked as she lowered the binoculars for a moment. She tried to reconcile the peaceful scene with the ominous feeling in her gut.

Vincent didn't respond with anything other than, "Keep watching."

She reluctantly lifted the binoculars again. The Black Guard marched the drones through the garden and past the pool. They led them toward the barren wasteland. Her heart pounded. She didn't know why, but she felt something terrible was about to happen.

The drones stood in front of a wide, open ditch. The Black Guard lined up in front of them and raised their rifles. Her breath caught in her throat. It couldn't be. It couldn't be as she feared. It just couldn't. The drones smiled, oblivious to the weapons pointed at them.

And then the guns fired.

The sound of rapid fire echoed across the wasteland. Selah screamed, but Ian quickly clamped his hand over her mouth. "They'll hear," he whispered urgently.

She saw the drones fall through the binoculars. Their heads and bodies were torn apart by the bullets. It didn't seem real. The people who had been promised relaxation and healing, who had trusted the Monarch to protect them, were now lifeless, discarded like broken toys. Some were kicked into the open pit, others dragged to an incinerator at the edge of the field.

She dropped the binoculars. Her hands trembled as she covered her face. She didn't want to cry, but she couldn't stop the tears. *Only bad drones cried.* The phrase mocked her. She heard it all her life, but now it had a horrible meaning. She had never imagined such cruelty. She had never thought the Monarch, who had promised to care for them, could do this.

Ian wrapped his arms around her, his voice soft but firm. "This is why we help drones. There isn't anyone else who can."

The weight of his words settled in her chest. He was right. The drones were so conditioned to trust, to obey, that even as they were led to their deaths, they believed the Monarch was their protector. They never suspected a thing.

She finally spoke after a long silence. Her voice raw. "Do they... do they go there right away? As soon as they arrive at the Institute?"

"No," Vincent replied quietly. "They're kept for a year. In limbo."

"Why a year?" She wiped her face. She was bombarded by images of her parents, of her grandmother. She remembered them entering the Institute, smiling, unaware of the fate that awaited them. Her tears continued.

"It gives the Monarch time to process their information, resolve their identifying codes. They use the drones' data for the archives, and then... they're sent to the Badlands."

Vincent's tone was grim. "We don't know how much of the information is kept, but we know some of it is destroyed."

Selah shuddered. "Are those men... the Black Guard?"

Vincent nodded. "Elite soldiers. They're not just guards. What you saw was a firing squad. They use real weapons, not like the fake guns they give the Justicemen for show. The Black Guard handles all executions."

"Why were there younger individuals? Were they Saboteurs?"

"No," Vincent sighed. "They just have more problems, like illnesses or chronic issues. If you aren't worth the resources, you don't get the resources. If you have a disease or ailment that isn't easily treated, you go to the 'institute.'"

Her stomach churned at the thought of real weapons being used against drones. "Drones wouldn't know what to do with weapons anyway," she muttered. She tried to comprehend the senseless slaughter she had just witnessed.

"True. But the Monarch fears drones more than you think."

Selah frowned. "Fears them? Why?"

He exhaled slowly. "Why do you think the Monarch controls every aspect of life? Why do they ration food, dictate healthcare, govern every moment of a drone's life? Because drones outnumber the Monarch Representatives and the Black Guard by the millions. If they ever realized their power, if they ever united, they could overthrow the entire system."

A cold chill ran down her spine. She had never thought of drones as having any real power. They were machines, programmed to obey. But now she realized they had been deliberately kept weak, deliberately pacified.

Vincent pulled out a white stick from his pocket and lit it. Selah stared at the strange item.

"What's that?" she asked.

"A cigarette," Vincent said. He exhaled a cloud of smoke. He handed her one, along with a lighter. "Here. It might help calm your nerves."

She hesitated, but Ian helped her light it. "Tobacco?" she asked, the word foreign in her mouth. "This isn't poison?"

Vincent laughed softly. "It's not good for you, but no, it won't kill you. Moderation is everything out here. Life is filled with pleasures of all kinds, but it's important to moderate your consumption of them. Most of the things considered poison in there are just lies from the Monarch."

She took a cautious drag. The bitter smoke filled her lungs. It was strange, not pleasant, but somehow it grounded her. She wasn't sure she liked it, but it gave her something to focus on besides the nightmare she just witnessed.

As they left, Vincent handed her a bottle of clear liquid. She took a sip. It burned like fire down her throat. "What is this?" she coughed.

"Vodka," Vincent replied with a smirk. "Alcohol."

She blinked. Alcohol. Another forbidden substance in Atlis. And yet, here she was, drinking it. Just like the cigarette, it didn't kill her. The Monarch's lies seemed endless.

Her mind buzzed with unanswered questions as they rode back to the city. Did her parents know? Did they realize what was happening in the end? Or did they, like the others, smile and believe they were going to be cared for, right up until the moment they were shot?

The journey back felt longer, heavier. She had seen the truth now. The Monarch wasn't a protector. It was a machine built on lies. It was fueled by fear and violence. And for the first time, she realized just how much had been hidden from her.

By the time they arrived back in Fortune City, all she wanted was to cleanse herself of the day. She took her time in the shower. She let the hot water wash over her.

Here, there were no limits. No one monitored her water usage. She had no fear of being scolded for indulging in a basic comfort. But even as the water ran over her skin, the image of the drones standing in front of the ditch wouldn't leave her mind.

The Monarch had taken everything from her. Her family, her friends, her identity. It lied to her and convinced her that its way was the only way, that life outside its control was chaos and destruction.

But now she knew better.

CHAPTER 33

"How long have you been planning this?" Trajan asked. His voice bounced off the damp concrete walls.

"A while..." Marcus replied without looking back. "Longer than I care to admit."

"You seem pretty sure of where we're going," Trajan pressed. "Too sure."

Marcus glanced over his shoulder. His expression unreadable in the flickering lantern light. "You'd rather I didn't know what I was doing?"

"That's not what I'm saying," Trajan muttered. His voice tight. "It's just... this feels too easy now. Like they're letting us through. Where did they go?"

Marcus stopped abruptly and turned to face him. "You think this is easy?" he asked, his voice low but sharp. "You think I don't know the risks? That I haven't spent years studying these tunnels, figuring out how to stay one step ahead?"

"I'm not questioning your work," Trajan said, though doubt still gnawed at him. "I'm questioning the system. What if they already know? What if they're using us?"

Marcus's jaw tightened. "If you're that paranoid, turn back. But I'm not stopping."

He hesitated. His pulse pounded in his ears. Then he followed Marcus deeper into the tunnels. He couldn't turn back now. Whatever awaited them ahead, success, failure, or death, was better than the suffocating existence he left behind.

They came across another massive chamber several hours later. Its walls were lined with rusted machinery and corroded pipes. The air was thick with the scent of oil and decay, and the faint hum of electricity vibrated through the floor. He wiped sweat from his brow.

"Let's rest a moment," Marcus said. He leaned against an ancient pillar. His movements had slowed. Weariness had stolen their speed and determination.

Trajan nodded and dropped onto a cold metal grate. He pulled out a water flask. He took a long sip before he passed it to Marcus. The silence felt heavier here, as if the tunnel itself held its breath.

"Why do you want to end it?" Trajan asked. "I've lost 4 wives to the Monarch. Why do you want to destroy him?"

"Because it's evil. You know, my father made me fight my brother to get his position. I didn't want to. I didn't care. I loved my brother. But father couldn't have that. He didn't want his children to love each other, but to kill each other. We were best friends... until that last year. We were 19 and 20. Father filled his head with lies for that last year. By the time it was over, he had tried every way he could to kill me. Father drummed it into his head that I wanted to assassinate him."

Marcus looked down. Tears welled in his eyes, "He finally came at me with a knife. I tried not to fight... to go with peace because he was my brother. It didn't work out like that. He landed on the knife he was going to use on me. And that is how I got this wonderful position." His words dripped with bitter sarcasm.

They didn't say more for a time. Every muscle in his body ached. It felt like they'd ran the gauntlet for a year. He leaned his head back against the wall and sighed.

Suddenly, a foreign sound began. He looked at Marcus. A faint, high, pitched whine grew louder, like a machine powered up. Trajan froze. "Do you hear that?"

Marcus straightened, his eyes narrowing. "Yeah. Something's, "

The tunnel flooded with harsh white light and blinded them both. A deafening alarm blared. Its shrill cry reverberated off the walls. His heart leapt into his throat as metallic clanging echoed from the corridors ahead and behind.

"They found us," Marcus hissed. His voice was barely audible over the cacophony.

"No kidding!" Trajan shouted, pulling his knife from his belt. "How the hell did they know?"

Marcus didn't answer. His face was a mask of grim determination as he grabbed Trajan's arm and pulled him toward the nearest exit. The clanging grew louder, accompanied by the unmistakable sound of boots pounding against metal.

"Run!" Marcus barked. They sprinted into a side tunnel with the alarm still blaring.

The tunnel twisted and turned. The flickering lantern casting erratic shadows that seemed to reach for them. Trajan's lungs burned as they ran. The sound of pursuit was closing in behind them.

They rounded a corner and came face, to, face with a squad of Black Guards. Their armored forms blocked the path ahead. The guards raised their rifles. Their visors gleamed under the harsh lights.

"Get down!" Marcus shouted. He shoved Trajan to the floor. The guards opened fire. The sharp crack of their weapons deafening in the confined space. He rolled to the side. His knife glinted as he lunged at the nearest guard.

The blade found its mark. It slipped between the seams of the guard's armor. The man crumpled. His weapon clattered to the ground. Trajan grabbed it. The unfamiliar weight felt comforting in his hands. He turned and fired. The recoil jarred his arm as another guard fell.

Marcus fought with brutal efficiency. His movements were fluid and precise. He dispatched two guards in quick succession. His stolen blade flashed in the chaos. The remaining guards hesitated. Their formation broke under the unexpected resistance.

"This way!" Marcus shouted. He grabbed Trajan and pulled him toward another tunnel.

They ran again. The sound of pursuit faded as they put distance between themselves and the guards. His breath came in ragged gasps. His heart pounded as they stumbled into another chamber. The walls here were smooth and metallic. The air was colder, cleaner.

"What the hell was that?" Trajan demanded, rounding on Marcus. "How did they find us?"

Marcus didn't meet his gaze, his jaw clenched. "I don't know."

Trajan stared at him, his chest heaving. "You don't know, or you won't tell me?"

Marcus's silence was answer enough.

CHAPTER 34

She wasn't ready for another trip to Atlis, but whispers of a new venture already swirled among the group. This time, they aimed to liberate a larger number of ex, drones, with a risky operation that seemed doomed from the start. How could they possibly smuggle out so many without exposing the underground network?

The more she listened to the discussions, the more her head throbbed. The logistics, the danger, it was too much. She could barely grasp the enormity of what they were up against.

The horrors of the Monarch's rule, which she'd been sheltered from in Atlis, unraveled before her. Over the past decade, there had been mass cleansing operations across the colonies. In Division H alone, over 50,000 had been killed, silently euthanized in their showers while the colony slept. Their bodies were whisked away under the cover of night to leave no trace of the atrocity.

The motives for the killings appeared to be resources. Whenever the Colony Order encountered years of famine or drought, drones had to die to ensure resources were plentiful.

Seven years ago, a suspected anti, Monarch conspiracy in Division B had resulted in the execution of 5,250 drones, and that was just a fraction of the slaughter. The majority of the records were erased before they could be counted.

Beyond Atlis, the scale of death was even more staggering. In Estilium, the colony across the sea, 2 million drones were annihilated in the past year. In Hibietova, an entire continent away, female drones were removed from labor and forced into becoming Monarch Breeders. In Etron, 45,000 male drones had been exterminated in just five years to make way for more females.

The carnage had been so extreme that now the colonies were in panic because too many had been killed to sustain their size. The Monarch Representatives were as corrupt and useless as they were inept and incompetent.

The weight of these revelations bore down on her, especially as she learned of the world outside Atlis. The names of places, strange, yet oddly familiar, spoke of an ancient past, a time before the Monarch reshaped reality.

Her colony, Atlis, was vast, and spanned a good portion of what was once called North America. The Monarch claimed the area that stretched from the icy northern edges of Canada to a place that had been called Tennessee in a bygone world. Westward, the old territories extended as far as a place once known as Illinois.

She had been raised to believe this was the extent of the world, Atlis, the all, encompassing bastion of order and civilization. But now, in Fortune City, she learned of Hibietova, the western colony, stretching from what had once been Alaska down to Arizona, with Hawaii reserved exclusively for Monarch Representatives.

Then there was Etron... once known as South America. Arand encompassed what had been northern Europe. The world she had known was a fraction of the vastness the Monarch controlled.

Ancient civilizations, she was taught, were brutish and primitive, mere apes fumbling toward thought. That was the reason drones were considered inferior, half, evolved, incapable of true art or culture, nothing more than slightly intelligent animals at the mercy of the Monarch. But now, she realized the lie. The "stupid primitives" had built the very thing the drones worshipped, the everlasting Monarch.

As her mind drifted back to the Badlands. A fresh wave of anger and sorrow hit her. Her parents had been thrilled to retire. They had spoken so highly of the Institute of Longevity. It was the culmination of their hard work and dedication to the Monarch.

They believed they were going to be rewarded, to live in peace and comfort for the rest of their lives. If only she had known. Even if she had, though, would it have mattered? They were so loyal to the system, so blinded by their devotion, they never would have believed her.

And then, a year later, they would have been marched out through the gardens, past the lush hedges, to the barren Badlands beyond. The same fate awaited them as it did the criminals of Atlis, the Saboteurs, execution without dignity, without warning.

She couldn't stop thinking of the drones she left behind. How much did they know? Did her Floor Supervisor, the one who watched over her daily, understand the real purpose of the system? What about the forepersons at work, or the drones who administered the Institute of Wellness? Were they all as oblivious as she had been, or did they know just enough to keep themselves in line?

She descended into quiet as she walked down to supper alone. The din of conversation from the other room barely registered. Ian, Vincent, and the others were deep in planning. Their voices rose and fell with the excitement of a new mission.

She didn't care to join. Why would she? She had already escaped the Monarch's grasp twice, and tempting fate again felt like a fool's errand. She wanted to hide, but she didn't want to do so alone.

She absently picked at her food at the table. Her appetite had waned. It was replaced with the gnawing feelings of helplessness.

The talk of further rebellion, of freeing more drones, it sounded noble in theory, but in reality, it was impossible. She knew the walls, the security, the omnipresent watchfulness of the system. How could a few escapees make any real difference against a force that had dominated for centuries?

Her mind spiraled. Would the Monarch ever truly be defeated? Or was the fight a hopeless battle, one that would end with more bodies in the Badlands, more lives lost to the endless slaughter? The thought brought a wave of exhaustion over her. She didn't have the energy to think about it, much less engage in their plotting.

Let them talk. Let them plan. She had escaped, and that was enough. For now.

CHAPTER 35

She rose from her bed and dressed in another set of clothes. The shopping trip with Rose the previous evening was a success. She now had several new outfits to choose from.

It was a strange feeling, picking her own clothes. She couldn't even recall having to make decisions before the fog, but she was getting better at it. The fear of poor choices had lessened. No one here scolded you for choosing the wrong thing.

She headed downstairs to the dining area for breakfast. The smell of fresh eggs and bacon greeted her. She still wasn't accustomed to the smell of freshly made bacon. She smiled softly and inhaled deeply. Her newfound freedom was a precious thing.

She decided on eggs, bacon, and some buttered toast. As she moved to find a seat, she noticed Martha, one of the city's oldest Elders, sitting alone. That was unusual. Martha was almost always surrounded by people seeking her wisdom.

Selah approached. "Is no one sitting with you?"

"Not yet," Martha replied with a warm smile. "Have a seat, my dear."

They exchanged pleasantries. They talked about the weather and the simple pleasures of Fortune City. When their food arrived, Selah picked at her eggs. She'd tried scrambled eggs the day before, so today she opted for an omelet. She still marveled at how different food was here, how rich and flavorful it could be, free from the bland, synthetic taste of the rations in Atlis.

Martha's sharp eyes rested on her. "You must have so many questions."

Selah hesitated. "I do... I don't know where to start."

Martha chuckled softly. "It's always overwhelming at first. Most of us here have been where you are now."

"Were you in Atlis?" Selah asked, her voice low, almost hesitant.

"No, never," Martha shook her head. "I was born and raised right here in Fortune City."

Selah blinked in surprise. "You've never been in Atlis?" It seemed impossible. She had assumed everyone had come from the colonies. "But... how were you made?"

Martha dropped her fork and broke into hearty laughter. The happy sound filled the room. She blushed when she felt every pair of eyes turn toward her. She hadn't meant to ask anything funny. "I'm sorry," she whispered. "Was I not supposed to ask?"

Martha wiped a tear from the corner of her eye, still smiling. "Oh, my dear, you delight me. No, no, you can ask whatever you like. Sometimes a question just takes me by surprise, that's all."

Selah tried to hide her embarrassment by taking a bite of toast. The heads around them finally turned away. Martha leaned in slightly. "I was naturally conceived."

Selah furrowed her brow. "Conception occurs in a Petri dish." She lowered her voice, as if the notion were scandalous.

Martha smiled and shook her head. "No, dear. Conception happens naturally, between a man and a woman."

That answer stunned Selah. "Naturally? Without intervention?" She paused. Her mind raced from the possibilities. "And you were born healthy?"

"Perfectly," Martha said. Her eyes still twinkled with amusement.

She didn't know what to say. The idea that people could create life without the Monarch's intervention seemed impossible. Everything about the world outside the colony was so different, so... free.

"How is it possible for people to create life without intervention?" Selah finally asked. Curiosity overrode her hesitation.

"Oh, I'm not the best person to explain it," Martha chuckled. "It's been many years since I've had to worry about that sort of thing."

"If drones can conceive naturally, why does the Monarch interfere?" Selah pressed.

Martha's smile faded slightly. "Control. Controlling the population means controlling the people. The Monarch controls every aspect of life in the colonies. By eliminating natural conception, they ensure they decide who gets to live and when. If drones reproduced naturally, there would be too many, and they would start to think for themselves. The Monarch can't allow that."

Selah's mind reeled at the implications. "So, they eliminate... gender?"

Martha nodded. "Yes, they suppress it. Drones are given injections that prevent fertility in women and lower the... urges in men. It's all part of keeping the population manageable."

Selah thought for a moment. "Isn't it easier to genetically alter drones to stop reproduction?"

"No," Martha said, "that's far too risky and expensive. Surgeries and genetic modifications can fail, and there are always side effects. Chemicals are cheaper, easier, and more effective."

"So... I'm neutered?" Selah said, the unfamiliar term sounding foreign on her tongue. The Monarch had never explained such things.

"When was your last check, up?" Martha asked.

Selah replied. "They canceled my appointment around a month ago. I ran out of vitamins and came out of the fog."

Martha said with a kind smile. "The doctors here can help you with that if you need it. It's something they know a lot more about than I do."

"What urges do men have? Why are they the only ones?"

Martha again encouraged her to discuss everything with their doctors, but she wasn't sure she wanted to. She still didn't understand what urges were, or why men had them. The urge to kill? Did nature instill in them an urge to risk life and limb on impossible missions?

Selah smiled back and decided not to press the issue. She felt a warmth spread through her. It was amazing to speak to someone so full of wisdom, someone who had lived outside the Monarch's grasp for so long. Martha hadn't been ushered away to the Institute of Longevity. She was here, alive and vibrant, able to share her knowledge with the younger generation.

She decided to take a walk after breakfast. She hadn't explored Fortune City alone and today seemed like the perfect time. The town was small, at least on the surface, but Ian had told her that much of it lay underground. The tallest building was five or six stories. It was nothing like the towering monoliths of Atlis that stretched endlessly into the sky.

The simple pleasure of walking outside at her own pace, without a destination, filled her with a sense of peace. Back in the colonies, drones weren't allowed to wander. They walked to work, to the Salute, or nowhere at all. Here, the sky was blue, the sun was warm, and the air felt clean. She didn't have to worry about wasting resources or being watched every second.

Her thoughts wandered back to the Badlands. She could still hear the gunshots. The sharp crack as bullets tore through flesh. The memory made her shudder, but she couldn't shake it. Those drones had smiled, oblivious to their fate. Did they even know to fear what was happening? Or had the Monarch stolen that from them too?

As she continued, she came across an unusual building. This one had a pointed turret that stretched high above the rest, unlike the others. It was topped with a metal cross. She curiously approached and knocked on the large wooden doors. When no one answered, she knocked again, louder this time.

Finally, she pushed one of the doors open and peeked inside. "Hello?" she called.

The interior was unlike anything she'd seen before. Long wooden benches stretched out in rows, which led to a raised platform at the front. A tall cross stood behind the platform, and on either side of it were two open doors.

"Hello?" a male voice with a strange accent called from one of the side rooms.

Selah walked cautiously forward. She peeked into the left room. An older man was polishing a set of silver ceremonial dishes. He smiled when he saw her. "Ah, hello there, my dear. Sorry, I didn't hear you knock."

"What is this place?" she asked, her curiosity piqued.

"This is a church," he replied. "It's where we come to worship God."

He sat the cloth and the dish down. "Are you a refugee?" She nodded as he approached her. "Come, let's sit, and have a nice talk."

"You have a strange accent." She hoped she didn't offend him by pointing it out, but he did. They walked to the nearest bench and sat down.

"Yes, I'm originally from England, or the Arand Colony as you might know it. You can call me Rev. Baker."

"I'm Selah. You're from Eng... land?"

"I fled the Monarch's extension into England, an island off the continent of Europe. I eventually wound up here, in Fortune City. It's a lovely town."

"I'm from Atlis."

"I gathered as much. This is a church."

"A church?"

"It's where we worship God."

"Worship God? You mean religion?"

"Yes."

"Religion is illegal."

"Yes, indeed, it's illegal in the colonies. Although, I'm sure you were warned against religion and faith."

"Faith?"

"Faith is when you believe in something unseen, because you feel it's the right thing to do. Religion is not something that adheres to the individual, or their whims, but makes you want to represent its truths. It makes you a better person."

"Things unseen don't exist... at least they didn't. I guess we worshipped the Monarch."

"I know. Many in my family did, too. Once upon a time, people believed the wind to be magic. It's unseen, but we have tools to measure it. There is much in our world we still don't have the technology to study and dismissing it because we're primitive is no different than proclaiming the world is flat."

"You seem harmless," she spoke as they sat on the bench nearest the front. "Why was religion so bad?"

"It became an easy target for the woes of the world. Religion is a threat to government. It is a threat to control. It is a threat to the Monarch. The governments of the world could no more disprove there was a God than they could prove their leaders were divinely chosen by God. So, they removed all mention of him. They began anti, religious propaganda that said religion made people violent or evil, somehow. In reality, human nature is often violent and evil. Mankind needed to eliminate God so they could take his place. When they became gods, their governments could become gods."

"Why didn't they just rewrite it?"

"They did... to a point, which is why there are Monarch Temples."

"I mean why not leave the religions that were in existence and just rewrite those."

"Most major religions had been around for millennia or more. You can't rewrite something like that. Every time they tried to defame or belittle a faith, based figure, another emerged. So, they decided that to thwart future martyrs, they would simply eliminate religion and begin anew."

"Unsuccessfully?"

"You can never get rid of religion. Humans are innately spiritual. So, since you can't abolish faith or spirituality, you just move the object of adoration. After a few decades, established faith fled the colonies and all that remained worshipped the Monarch."

"Why did the world become as it is? Were there always Monarchs?"

"Not entirely. There were many societal and governmental systems in the world. Capitalism came to the forefront in the Twentieth Century; however, it was a human system and imperfect. So, world leaders decided to try Socialism. It gave them more control over the populations. But, again, it is another failed endeavor, as any system from mankind is. Then, it was decided to move towards Communism, which offered even greater control, yet led to more failure."

"Then came the Monarch?"

"Eventually. World leaders wanted a way to eliminate crime and, while it was a lofty ambition, it ignored the primary reason for crime."

"Poverty?"

"Humanity. Humans are deeply complex creatures. Every individual is a combination of light and dark. Every person has a propensity to commit a crime or to achieve great things. The only way a system could eliminate crime was to eliminate humans. Monarch engineers tried to cut it out, push it back, but it was impossible. Then, they figured out how to snuff it out with drugs. They 'defeated' poverty the same way. They convince the drones that slavery is freedom, and table scraps are a feast. Luxury foods, such as meat or chocolate, are labelled as poison so drones aren't tempted to try them, even if they encounter them."

"Being a drone has a tremendous price tag." She softly said, more to herself than him.

"Yes, it does." He smiled. "They want to kill the human being as a whole. We weren't meant to live without poverty or crime. It's unnatural. We can't live without sickness or pain. They're integral parts of life. Passion and individuality are strengths, not weaknesses. Some people turned to crime, or did horrific things because of their issues, but only a few. Those horrible aspects of life are meant to make us more than just humans. No great invention or achievement in history has ever come about without a problem fueling the discovery. Life in the colonies isn't life, it's simply existence."

"What happened then?"

"It was decided that humans were too incompetent to choose any government or even devise one. A group of global leaders came together and decided to enforce the Monarch."

"Was it a fast change?"

"Most definitely. It was planned for some time, and they used highly creative orchestration. Technology was used to alienate individuals from one another. People began to prefer the company of screens to that of other people. That was the first step."

"They turned them into drones?"

"Sort of. Much of the population became obsessed with their self, importance and popularity on those screens. People were much more controllable when the powers, that, be could punish them, even for simply saying the wrong things."

"Like the Institute of Clarity?"

"Exactly."

"Then, they targeted religion. If your faith didn't follow society's wishes, you were bad. You were ignorant or hated science, even if you didn't. You were afraid... or hated others. The malevolent propaganda had one purpose: to take away all distractions from the ruling class.

"They robbed humanity of hope, and of what brought them comfort. After a few decades of sedation, people accepted that the Monarch was their hope. Originally, science was science, not a tool for bigotry. During the Twentieth Century, it seemed to lose that original purpose. It became a substitute for, or some strange rival to, religion."

"So, there was a difference between the two?"

"Indeed. During that same century, science was used as a platform for racial superiority. It went from being a tool used for one form of intolerance to another."

"We're taught the Monarch destroyed slavery during that century."

"No, slavery didn't exist in that century. The slavery of drones did, but not the traditional slavery."

"So, it wasn't all bad?"

"Certainly not. There were many notable, genuinely good accomplishments from the era. Humanity just couldn't stop itself from returning to barbarism. Humans are a funny lot. Instead of throwing rocks or bullets at neighbors, they used words to stir public hatred against them. Politics became an excuse for violence and animosity, for threats and intimidation, as opposed to a simple civic process that free people enjoyed. Business owners could speak, and if their words were deemed inappropriate, the world could destroy them."

"Why does your God allow this world?"

"God is benevolent enough to let humans have the world they create. He doesn't grant wishes upon request. Death, as we see it, is a horrible tragedy. God knows it's merely a transformation. Humanity was given knowledge and power to make the world better. What they do with it is their responsibility. Humans are agents of free will.

He leaned back and continued, "I believe the Monarch was allowed to come to power, for no other reason than to show humanity what terror and brutality it's capable of. Sadly, every few generations that are blessed enough to avoid major tragedy or disaster, becomes arrogant. They believe they're better than their ancestors, kinder, gentler, or more intelligent. They aren't. Every generation is just as flawed and fallible as the last, and education doesn't sway human tenacity for evil.

"The barbarism of murder simply evolved to barbarism of slander and then back to murder when society reverted. Since humans are headstrong, they develop the same negative qualities as their ancestors. It just manifests in different ways, but the same negative consequences occur repeatedly. It shocks every generation it strikes, but in reality, its history repeating itself. The Monarch offered the world a new start once it toppled."

"Maybe we don't deserve more than that."

"That's not a statement we can make. We can't say who deserves what. Humans deserve the chance to prove their worth. They deserve to feel and to hope. They deserve a chance to make the world better, not just to exist until the Monarch decides it's time for them to die."

"What happened in the new start?"

"It was imperative for governments to disarm the people. That ensured they were defenseless. Who can help you when your government has all the weapons? This was done through a few well, orchestrated tragedies that involved. It was all that was necessary to turn the population against weapons altogether. The Monarch, of course, never relinquished its arms. The War of Arms happened then."

"I remember that... I think."

"You probably do. It just ended a couple of decades ago.

The conversation continued of the Monarch's rule and how any God allowed it. Of how humans wanted domain but then looked for a scapegoat when they destroyed that domain. She started out of the sanctuary with her mind in turmoil. Everything went against everything what she was taught. *A god that didn't force you to follow him.*

She'd never considered the effect it would have on her. Could such an entity exist? In Atlis, you followed the Monarch. There was no question, because if you doubted or questioned, you were a saboteur. Drones could be saboteurs and not even know it.

They were taught there was no intelligent design at creation, for there was no other power in the universe like the Monarch. Man came from a fluke, an accident, a mere coincidence. He was no deity, no reflection of any deity, just look at how flawed humans were. Wasn't that proof that they descended from apes?

Or was it as simple as Baker suggested? A supreme power orchestrated life. Was that idea really any more far, fetched than an innumerable series of perfect coincidences, which were perfectly timed, in an imperfect world?

The reverend nodded. "Yes, it is in the colonies. But here, we're free to believe and worship as we choose."

The rest of the conversation flowed naturally from there. Reverend Baker succinctly explained the history of the church, the rise of the Monarch, and humanity's struggle to maintain their connection to something greater than themselves.

She eventually left the church and rejoined Ian. She found herself filled with even more questions, but also a growing sense of determination. There was an entire world outside of Atlis, a world she was just beginning to discover.

Ian caught up with her. "You want to see your new home?"

"Very much." She followed his lead.

They walked to a cluster of trees behind the hotel building. It looked like an old mine of some sort. Broken boards were nailed up and a faded "Do Not Enter" sign was crooked. The boards were actually a spring, hinged gate. They walked inside and he pushed open another boarded, up entrance. "These access points are all over the town."

They descended a series of metal and concrete steps until they came to a large door. "This goes down about 20 feet." He pushed the large metal door, and they walked inside.

She stood for a moment. A large cobble, stone walkway appeared to go on forever. Countless stores and shops lined either side of the street. Massive skylights poured sunlight down into the subterranean realm. "It's beautiful." She whispered.

"Yes, it is. Most of the skylights are set beneath thick glades of trees, plus they're coated with a non, reflective substance. The Monarch can fly those jets over all day and never see them, even in winter."

People rode bicycles over the beige cobbles and walkways. The sidewalks were paved with cream, colored tiles. It was a strange place, but it was wonderful. Rich scents of food filled the air. "Do people live down here?"

Bicycles were luxuries in Atlis. Only Monarch Representatives had them. Drones seldom saw them. The average drone was far too accident, prone, and the devices were too expensive to give everyone. Down here, they were everywhere.

"Yes, they sure do. Their houses are built into the ground just like these stores."

"How big is this place?"

"About 36 square miles. We're right under the surface so we don't have to worry about cave, ins or the dangers of tunneling. Since its underground, everything is naturally insulated. Underground spaces are cheaper and easier to heat and cool."

"What was this place?"

"It was a zinc mine long ago. Those who fled the Monarch discovered them. We have a functional subway system here, about four miles over."

"Where does it go?"

"Anywhere. This is Newsouth. You can take the subway and go down into Seminole. That used to be called Florida. You can go west into the plains area, to Ozarkadia. Beyond that is Calificia."

"Does the Monarch know about it all?"

"No. We can't let the Monarch know this is down here."

"How can so much exist so secretly?"

"It's fairly easy. The Monarch broke up the global communications industries quickly. You can't control people who freely access information. You take the outside information away and people are dependent on the government for it."

"It doesn't exist at all?"

"They have their systems, we have our systems, and so far, the two have never interfered with one another."

One of the most striking features of this new world was the people. She'd never witnessed people with so many unusual colors. "Why are people here so colorful?"

"They're different races, and some are different ethnicities."

"Why do they look so different?"

"The Monarch mixes all races together. The best way to eliminate racial distinctiveness is to combine all races. A drone father seldom has offspring with his cells. Usually, the Monarch chooses a biological father to fertilize the mother's cells, who isn't the father unit."

"Physical distinctiveness is against the Monarch's wishes."

"Precisely."

She noticed a bookstore ahead. "Is that what I think it is?"

"A bookstore? Sure is."

"We never have books... had, I should say."

"It's fine. You'll get used to it."

"Can I look at them?"

"Do whatever you like." He seemed amused by her questions. She didn't want to amuse him, but she didn't care. The point was that she was out of Atlis. She was away from the Monarch, and she was getting ready to enter a bookstore.

The Monarch never allowed printed books. Everything was onscreen because printed information created too much waste. Although it was probably more like printed words couldn't be changed.

She didn't know where to begin. The bookstore was two stories high. Sunlight poured in through a massive skylight above. There were facing chairs in each corner, a couch on the far side and all spaces in between were packed with books.

She'd always wanted a paper book. Something she could go back and read, or something she could carry with her. She wanted to touch the pages and the glossy colored covers.

"Hello?" A feminine voice called from a room in the back.

"Hello?" She answered, although she didn't know what to expect. Did humans here answer when called or did they wait for the individual to enter the room?

Ian walked strode towards the history section. A little woman emerged from the room in the back. She walked rapidly while a stack of hardcover books teetered in her arms. "Sorry, I was getting some books from the back."

"It's fine," she smiled.

"So, what can I help you with?" She scooted the stack onto a nearby table and turned. "What are you looking for?"

"I don't know. I've never seen a bookstore before. It's amazing."

"Are you from Atlis?" The older lady asked as if she'd been in the same situation a thousand times.

"Yes."

"I see. Okay, let's start from the beginning. Follow me." She walked rapidly back towards the same supply room. "You need to start with the basics. I have a few copies of history books you should probably read first. They were made long before the Monarch."

"How much are they?"

"We have a special stock for Atlis refugees. They're free."

"Really? Thank you."

"Tell me what you know of Shakespeare."

"I know he wrote *Romeo and Juliet* among other classics."

"Uh, huh. What was that about?"

"Juliet turned Romeo in as a saboteur, at the conclusion. She lives happily ever after serving the Monarch."

"Okay," she raised her brows behind her glasses. The dark lens made it nearly impossible to see her eyes. "You need to read the real thing." She picked up another paperback and handed it to her.

"So, it's not really like that?"

"Nothing in Atlis is really like that. Here's *1984*. Have you read that?"

"Winston explores his love for Big Brother, which was the Monarch."

"What about *Fahrenheit 451*?"

"Guy Montag went against the Monarch and tried to distribute books to drones. He winds up being taken to the Institute of Clarity."

"Gone with the Wind?"

"Scarlett O'Hara abandoned all she knew to become a devoted Breeder for the Monarch."

"Rebecca?"

"She turns Maxim in for being a Saboteur."

"Wow," she spoke. "Most drones don't remember the books they've read. You have an exceptional memory for literature. She crossed her arms, "What about the Holy Bible?"

"That's a religious book and religious texts are fuel for hatred." The woman finally introduced herself as Madge. She grabbed an old canvas bag from the coat hanger. "You'll need to carry all that. You need to read the real books."

"How do I repay you?"

"Never mind that. Anything I can do to undo what the Monarch does, especially in literature, is a reward in itself."

They returned to the front of the store. Ian was immersed in a large book discussing automobiles. She walked over to him, "I have plenty of reading material."

"Do you need me to get it?"

"No, Madge said it was free."

Ian waved at her. "She's sweet."

"I envy her, to work here, surrounded by all these books. I've always wanted to be around books, actual books. Not just the electronic texts used in Atlis."

Ian nodded toward the window with his chin. "Well, if you want to settle here in Newsouth."

A "Help Wanted" sign leaned against the bottom of the window. "I don't have the education to work with books."

"You don't need one, hon." Madge called behind her. She sounded out of breath as she scooted another stack of books onto the table. "You just need a good back."

"Do I need to fill out paperwork?"

"Is she in the system, Ian?" Madge looked at him.

"Yes, she was placed when her axiom was removed."

"Well, can you start tomorrow?"

She waited a moment. There had to be a punch line somewhere. She wasn't qualified to work with books. She didn't have any training. She only had a Monarch, grade education.

"I would love to," she spoke. Maybe they would ultimately turn her away, but she had to try. It was too wonderful. To work in a bookstore and see books all day had to be heaven.

They discussed the details and her pay before she left. No uniform was necessary. She felt giddy as they walked out. "I can't believe I'm working in a bookstore. I can't believe it."

Ian grinned at her jubilance. "You're amazing."

"Why?"

"You embrace this new life such enthusiasm. Most drones need time to function normally. They come to us terrified. A number refused to leave their rooms for days. Their desire to leave the Monarch is all that saves them."

"I want to be here. To be out of Atlis."

"You are."

CHAPTER 36

They wandered through the underground city of Newsouth for hours. She took in the sights and marveled at the architecture. She couldn't believe what she was seeing. The underground park was a masterpiece, with towering trees, lush greenery, and even a waterfall that cascaded over twenty feet down into a shimmering pool.

A natural stream wound its way through the park, its waters cool and clear. It flowed naturally through the stone pathways. The sound of rushing water filled the air, a serene contrast to the constant hum of machinery she had known in Atlis.

"This is amazing," she said in awe, watching as the sunlight filtered through the artificial skylights above. "Whatever led them to make such a beautiful place?"

"Necessity," Ian replied, his voice carrying a tone of pride. "For a long time, no one believed we could have beautiful things. The Monarch destroyed every garden and green space that grew above ground. When cities tried to grow, they crushed them. So the people here learned to create beauty underground, where the Monarch couldn't reach."

"How many cities like this are there?" she asked, still marveling at the new underground world.

"More than you'd think," Ian said. "Everywhere the colonies don't reach, there are cities like this, hidden. We've got a network of subway systems and underground highways connecting them, all invisible to the Monarch."

"Do they have cars down here?" She asked. She tried to imagine what an underground highway might look like.

"Some, but we have to be cautious with vehicles. The Monarch is always watching, and anything that moves on a large scale gets their attention."

"Why does the Monarch care?" she wondered aloud. She still tried to wrap her mind around the control they exercised.

"Because they can't control it," Ian said simply. "Anything they don't control is a threat."

They explored more of the city as the day went on. They returned to the hotel as evening approached. She discovered the vibrant, spicy flavors of Mexican cuisine at dinner, tasting enchiladas, rice, and beans for the first time. She washed it down with a cold beer. She still marveled at how different life was now.

"The old life feels like a dream," she mused and swirled the amber liquid in her glass. "Like a nightmare, really."

"I know," Ian agreed. "I felt that way for a long time, too. Sometimes I still do."

They finished their meal with a sweet dessert of churros, the cinnamon and sugar coating a delicious contrast to the rich meal they had just enjoyed. She was full and content as they walked back to her room. The day's events swirling in her mind.

"Have you spoken with Vincent?" she asked once they were inside.

"I have," Ian said. His expression grew more serious. "They're preparing. The plan seems solid."

"What do they plan to do?"

"They're going to infiltrate Atlis. A group of fighters is coming in from other cities next week to help. The goal is to take control of Division T."

Her heart skipped a beat. "How could you overtake Atlis?"

"It's not Atlis, just a division. Whoever controls Division T controls the entire colony," he explained. "The drones aren't a threat. The Monarch hasn't trained them to fight. The key is to get into the division without notice. That's where our fighters come in. They'll use the jet entrance to infiltrate the division."

"Are you going?" The thought of Ian leaving filled her with dread. She couldn't bear the idea of losing him.

"Of course I'm going," he said, smiling faintly. "I can't let them go alone. Every pair of hands is needed."

"But... you can't leave me." The words came out before she could stop them. Her emotions surged, raw and unfiltered. She couldn't imagine him going off into battle, risking his life. Not after everything they'd been through.

"Selah," he said gently, "I can't let the Monarch grow stronger, not while there's breath in my body. We've waited too long already. It has to happen sooner or later. If we don't strike now, we'll lose our advantage."

"What if you get hurt?" Her voice trembled as she grabbed his hand. She held it tight. "What if you don't come back?"

"I'll come back," Ian promised, though the weight of his words hung heavy between them.

"I'll go with you," she declared. Her resolve solidified. She couldn't just stand by and wait. She was young, capable, and knew the ins and outs of the Monarch's system. She could help.

"No women are going." Ian said firmly. "You're not ready for that kind of danger. You just left Atlis, Selah. You're still recovering from everything the Monarch put you through. Your body isn't strong enough for the trauma of battle. We don't take women."

"Women can fight, too."

He gave her a somber smile. "It isn't a question of ability. It's our job to protect you, all of our ladies, and we can't do that and fight a potentially brutal battle."

"Why can't we even fight in the back?"

"Do you have any idea what would happen to female prisoners of war in the Colony Order? If we lost, you would not be released. You would be taken inside."

"I don't care," she snapped. Her voice rose. "If you're going, I'm going."

"No." He refused. "No, you aren't. Even if all those factors aren't considered, you're still weak. Your system is still adjusting. You haven't fully recovered yet."

"Why are you going, then? Why risk your life?" She couldn't hold back the tears that welled up in her eyes. She hated to cry. She hated to feel this vulnerable, but she couldn't stop it.

"Because we've planned this for a long time, and we're running out of time," Ian said softly. He wrapped his arm around her. "You have to trust me."

She leaned into him, her tears soaking into his shirt. "I trust you, but I don't trust the Monarch. They'll kill you."

"They'll kill us all if we don't do something," Ian said, his voice steady. "We either strike first, or we wait for them to come after us.

They're expanding. The jets that used to fly over once a month are flying over weekly now. They're spying on us, calculating their next move."

She wiped her eyes. She still heard the droning sound of the jets from earlier. The dark, ominous machines that passed overhead. "I can't lose you," she whispered, her voice breaking.

Ian kissed the top of her head. "My poor Selah," he said softly. "I know this is all overwhelming for you."

"It's not a war," she said. Her voice stronger now. "It's losing you. I can't lose you, Ian."

"I love you, Selah," he said, his voice filled with emotion. "I always have."

The words hung between them like a promise. Her heart leapt in her chest, and she kissed him. Her lips sought his in a desperate, urgent need. She didn't care about anything else, only this moment mattered.

They fell back onto the bed, their bodies entwined, the heat of the moment overtaking them. His hands roamed her body, and she felt alive in ways she had never experienced before. Every touch, every kiss made her heart race. Her mind spun with sensations she couldn't fully understand.

But then, as quickly as it had started, he pulled away. "We need to slow down," he said, his breathing heavy.

"Why?" Selah asked, confused. "I don't want to stop."

"It's too soon," Ian said gently. "You're not ready for this."

"I think I am," she insisted. "I'm here, aren't I?"

Ian laughed softly. His fingers tracing the edge of her face. "You'll understand when the time is right."

She felt a twinge of embarrassment. "What do you mean?"

"When two people love each other, there's a physical union," he said, his tone soft.

"A union?" she repeated. She didn't fully understand.

"Yes," Ian chuckled. "But it can lead to... consequences. Like getting pregnant."

Her eyes widened. "A baby? We could make a baby?" The thought filled her with hope. "A life untouched by the Monarch?"

"Yes," Ian said. "That's how it happens."

"I want to have your baby," she whispered. She rested her head against his chest. The idea filled her with a strange, thrilling excitement. "A new life. A life free from the Monarch."

A moment of silence later, he answered "You can't know that, yet."

"I'm in my third decade in life. I think I know what I want." She grew tired of feeling like a child. Everything in this new world, no matter how wonderful or beautiful, always implied she knew nothing. "I'm not a child and I'm not foggy headed. I know what I'm saying. I know what I want."

"I don't want to start a relationship, only to find out in a year or two that your heart is elsewhere. That's not fair to either one of us."

"My heart is right here."

"Right now... but what if you fall in love with someone else? You haven't met many people here and you may see someone you like even more."

"No one else helped me out of Atlis. No one else came to my rescue as you did. No one else helped me in my unit or helped me to avoid detection. No one here will have done that, either. No one else will have spent that first night away from Atlis with me."

He didn't answer. She didn't want to be second, guessed. She knew precisely what she wanted and if those choices carried consequences, then consequences be damned. She would embrace them.

The Monarch no longer dictated her life, nor would anyone else. She was her own responsibility now and that's what she wanted. The idea that she didn't know what she was saying or doing was insulting. She might be a former drone, but she wasn't stupid.

They lay in silence for a while. She didn't know what to say in the awkward stillness. She broke the uncomfortable quiet, "Everyone treats me like a child, Ian. I don't want you to do the same." She could take the treatment from everyone else. He was the one person she wanted to respect her choices.

"I don't think of you as a child."

"Then don't tell me what I'm going to do in a year or two. I didn't leave Atlis to have decisions made for me here, either."

Ian smiled but shook his head gently. "It's too soon for that, Selah. You're still learning about this new world."

"I know what I want," she said firmly. "And I want you."

They laid a moment longer and he kissed the crown of her head. For a moment, she thought he was somewhere far away. He lifted her chin again and kissed her mouth. He unleashed the same fervor he'd held earlier and took her breath. Again, she didn't want him to stop.

He removed her shirt and his own before she realized it. They were soon both nude. Her hands ran across his body as his did her own. She had never felt more alive before, more human.

She didn't understand what was happening, but she felt as if her body would burst into a thousand pieces. His touch did something to her. A short time later, she understood what was meant by union. They became as one. It felt like explosions occurred in her body, tremendous forces shifted, and the old world shattered in her heart.

This was what the Monarch wanted to destroy. The act came to a climax, and her body imploded against him. He followed soon after. They lay, gasping. Her mind sped with more thoughts and fears than she imagined. She curled up by his side. She felt so alive, so free.

"So that's the union," she smiled and looked up at him.

"Yes. Do you regret it?" He smiled but worry dimmed his eyes.

"Regret what?"

"The union."

"Why on earth would I do that?" They turned to face one another. "I'm happy... happier than ever."

"Did I hurt you?"

"Not at all. That was awesome."

He studied her a moment and finally smiled. "I'm glad I could be of service."

"Is it like that every time?"

"Yes."

They lay together in silence. Her body still buzzed with the emotions of the moment. Despite the fear of what was to come, there was hope. There was love. And for the first time in her life, she felt truly alive.

CHAPTER 37

He left to meet Vincent and the others early the next morning. She couldn't just let him go without doing something. She needed to act. After a quick breakfast, she made her way to find Rose. The only person she could trust with this plan. She found her sitting in the small park between the church and the clothing shop. She soaked in the peaceful morning.

"Thank you for meeting me," Selah said, and sat down beside her.

"What? Don't mention it," Rose replied. She stretched her arms out leisurely. "It's my day off anyway."

"I don't have to go into work until after lunch," Selah added. "Things are happening fast."

"Wow, that was fast. You already got a job?"

"Yes," Selah said with a small smile. "I'm working at the bookstore."

"I love Madge," Rose said with a grin. "She's a firecracker, isn't she?"

Selah's smile faded. Her thoughts returned to Ian. "I'm worried about Ian. I know what they're planning for next week, and I want to go with them. But he won't let me."

Rose glanced at her with raised eyebrows. "They're not letting any women go, Selah. It's too dangerous."

"I don't understand why. It feels like I'm being left behind."

"Because in war, women are too valuable," Rose said grimly, "but for the wrong reasons. In the old world, women caught in battle were enslaved for breeding. Not much has changed. If we're caught, they'll make us breeders, or worse, toys for the Black Guard. The Institute of Fertility in Atlis is there for a reason. Then, no one could ever get us out."

The gravity hit Selah hard. She had forgotten about the breeding initiatives in Atlis. "So there's really nothing we can do?"

"Actually..." Rose's voice dropped to a conspiratorial whisper, "I'm going. They just don't know it yet."

Selah's eyes widened. "What? How?"

"I'm a marksman," Rose said confidently. "I've been training for this. I'll teach you how to fire a sniper rifle, but you can't tell anyone, not even Ian. If they find out, they'll lock us down here."

Her heart raced with excitement and nervousness. "You'll teach me? But how will we go?"

"We'll follow from a distance," Rose explained. Her voice was calm. "We won't be in the thick of it. I'll teach you everything you need to know, how to shoot, how to stay hidden. We'll provide cover fire. Quiet and discreet."

Selah nodded. She felt a surge of determination. She hated going against Ian's wishes, but she knew she couldn't just sit by while he went off to fight. "I want to help," she said firmly. "I'll do whatever it takes."

Rose smiled. "Good. We probably won't be needed, but if we are, we'll be ready."

They made their way to a field outside the city. Rose opened a metal crate and handed Selah a sniper rifle. "It takes some getting used to," Rose said, helping her hold the gun properly. "But I think you'll do well."

Selah took a deep breath and aimed down the sight. Her first shot hit the target dead center.

Rose laughed in surprise. "You might have more talent than me."

"I hope we aren't needed." Selah said as she lowered the rifle, "but I want to be ready, just in case."

Rose went over the terrain. She taught her about landmarks and routes to take in case they had to retreat. She felt lost just a few miles out of Newsouth, but Rose knew every inch of the land.

They practiced for over an hour. The sound of gunfire faded into the quiet countryside. The conversation between them grew quieter as they prepared to head back.

"I wonder why everything's happening now," Selah mused aloud.

Rose shrugged. "The people who run the Monarch colonies are never satisfied. Their world is never enough. They want it all."

Selah frowned, her mind turning over what Rose had said. "Why can't they just leave the rest of the world alone?"

"They can't tolerate anyone else having even a hint of power," Rose explained. "The Monarch system thrives on control. If humanity exists outside the colonies, it shows that the Monarch isn't necessary. And they can't have that. It undermines their entire foundation."

"It's so pointless," Selah said with frustration. "What are they going to do once they've conquered everything? What's left after that?"

Rose shook her head, a dark smile playing on her lips. "I think you have to be one of them to understand. The Drones don't have a clue what's going on. It's the Monarch's inner circle, the people in Division 3, who are really pulling the strings."

"I don't want to see the head of the Monarch again," Selah said. She shivered at the memory. "I remember feeling like it was watching me."

"You must really love Ian to be willing to go back," Rose said softly.

"I do," Selah admitted, feeling a warmth in her chest. "I love him."

Rose smiled. "That's good. Because he loves you."

They returned to Fortune City after practice. Rose helped Selah pick out a few cosmetics at a nearby shop. They had lunch together, and then Rose taught her how to use the television in her room.

It was a simple thing, but Selah marveled at how different it was from the infoscreens in Atlis. Here, she could watch anything she wanted.

During a commercial break, Selah frowned at the screen. "What are those for?" she asked. It was an ad for feminine products.

Rose hesitated. "How much do you know about the female body, Selah?"

"Probably next to nothing." Selah answered, half, jokingly.

Rose took a deep breath. "Okay, this is going to be awkward, but here goes. I know no one else has talked to you about this, but someone needs to. You're going to start bleeding soon."

Selah's eyes widened. "Bleeding?"

Monarch

Rose nodded. "It's natural. It happens to women every month. It's part of your body's cycle. You've never experienced it because the injections they give Drones stop it."

"Why would I bleed? Does it hurt?"

"Sometimes," Rose admitted. "It's just how your body cleanses itself. The products in that commercial help keep it from staining your clothes."

Selah sat back, trying to absorb this new information. "Why don't drones have them?"

"The vitamins and injections suppress it," Rose explained. "But now that you're out of the system, your body will return to its natural state."

Selah's mind raced. "Does it have something to do with conception? Ian and I—"

Rose burst into laughter, cutting her off. "Whoa, whoa. Let's not get into that. That's a bit more than I needed to know."

Selah blushed but didn't regret speaking her truth. "I'm not ashamed. I made that choice."

"And you should be proud of it," Rose agreed, wiping away a tear of laughter. "But just be careful who you share it with. Not everyone's comfortable talking about such personal things."

Rose calmed a moment before she continued. "But, yes, it does relate to conception. It's just a way the female body cleans itself, more or less. If you want a detailed explanation, we have doctors to provide them."

"Okay. Thank you for letting me know."

"No one told me anything and I absolutely freaked out when I began to bleed. I thought I was dying."

She felt her eyes grow large, but Rose quickly added. "No, no, no. It's nothing to do with death. It's just a simple biological function. It doesn't mean anything other than your body is healthy."

She felt better after Rose assured her. She didn't want to start *bleeding*. It sounded horrible. She wasn't sure how much of a natural state she wanted to return to.

The rest of the day passed quickly. Her shift at the bookstore was easy. She helped organize the shelves while Madge dealt with customers.

She was learning so much about the literary world, the real literary world. It was a world she never imagined existed. Drones were taught that the Old World was filled with savagery and ignorance, but the books she was discovered told a different story.

By the time she returned to the hotel that evening, she was tired but fulfilled. Ian had spent the day working on construction across the city. They worked on a housing expansion in several other tunnels. He arrived at her door freshly showered, and they sat on the bed together. They talked about their day.

"I'm reading *1984*," she said. "I hope Winston escapes Big Brother the way we escaped the Monarch."

Ian smiled. "I won't spoil the ending for you."

They talked for a while longer, but the weight of the coming week hung over them. War was looming. The thought of losing Ian gnawed at her heart. She had finally found something real, something beautiful, and now it was being threatened.

As she lay in bed that night, she curled up next to him. The ache in her stomach returned. She hoped it was just from lifting too many books earlier. But deep down, she knew it was more than that. It was fear of the unknown, fear of losing the one person who had made her feel truly alive. She didn't want to think about the future. Not beyond this week.

CHAPTER 38

The week passed quickly. Every day, while Ian worked, her schedule was packed. Rose was relentless in preparing her for what was to come. They trained hard and worked on building strength and stamina. She had also learned how to ride a horse. That skill was essential for the journey along the mountain ridges, where they'd stay hidden.

"We'll need to travel high above," Rose explained during one of their rides. Her face was flushed from the crisp mountain air. "The Justicemen could be anywhere, within the borders of Atlis or outside them. We can't risk being seen."

She nodded and gripped the reins a little tighter. The steep peaks and rough terrain made her uneasy, but she knew the mountains were their only option. The more distance they kept between themselves and the colony, the safer they'd be.

She admired Rose's confidence. No one else could know about their plan, not Madge, not Ian, not anyone. The secrecy weighed on her, but she accepted it as necessary.

In truth, the secrecy was especially hard when it came to Ian. She spent each evening with him. They explored foods she had never even known existed. They laughed together, indulged in new experiences, and the once, isolating world of Fortune City began to feel more like home.

In the back of her mind, she felt the guilt growing. She couldn't tell him about her plan, not when she knew he'd run straight to Vincent and the others to stop her.

Perhaps it was right that they tried to protect the women from this. The danger for them was different from that of the men. Men might face death or torture in war, but for women, the threat was far worse.

If caught, they would be forced into breeding camps, subject to horrors she couldn't even fully comprehend. Vincent had suggested that Monarch Representatives were experimenting with new methods of fertilization, perverse manipulations of what should have been a beautiful act. She shuddered at the thought.

Her mind spun every evening, as she lay next to Ian, thinking of all she was learning. She laughed to herself as she recalled some of the words she'd learned, "orgasm" and "totalitarianism" among them. The vocabulary of her new life was rich and strange, filled with concepts she had never encountered in Atlis.

Yet, despite all this growth and discovery, there was always that gnawing fear. It could all be ripped away in a heartbeat. Ian might not come back from the mission. She and Rose might be captured. The peaceful life of Fortune City could be destroyed.

She tried to shake off her misgivings. *I can't refuse to go*, she thought. *Ian won't. Vincent won't. Rose won't.* Yet she found herself wrestling with her own courage. Why did she feel so weak? Why couldn't she be brave like the others? Perhaps she wasn't made for this life outside Atlis. Maybe, no matter how far she ran, she was still destined to be a drone.

But despite her doubts, Ian was supportive. He helped her settle into an apartment near his own. He helped her learn how to manage money and budget for the things she needed. It was a world away from the controlled environment of Atlis, where the Monarch handled everything, from food to bills to clothing.

Now, she had the freedom to shop for herself, to choose what she wanted. There was a simple pleasure in it, even in buying small treats for herself. She was making far more money at the bookstore than she ever did in the colony, and with her unused savings from Atlis, she had more than enough to live comfortably.

He suggested she stay with Rose while he was gone, and she agreed. And yet, the unease gnawed at her. She hated the secrecy, hated the lies, even if they were only by omission.

In Atlis, everything had been hidden. Every truth was buried beneath layers of deception. She had sworn never to live that way again. And yet, here she was, hiding her plans from Ian, the one person she trusted more than anyone.

As the day crept closer, the feeling in her gut only grew stronger. She had to go. Something inside her told her that if she didn't, tragedy would strike. It was a pull she couldn't ignore, like an invisible hand guiding her toward the unknown. She knew that if she stayed behind and something terrible happened, she'd never forgive herself. The guilt would consume her.

If things went wrong, if Ian died, if Rose was captured, she wouldn't be able to live with herself. She'd rather walk up to the gates of Atlis and let t hem kill her, than carry the burden of knowing she could have acted and didn't.

As the last day approached, she felt the weight of what was to come. The decision had been made. She would go, no matter what. There was no turning back now.

CHAPTER 39

Selah didn't expect to be so emotional when Ian walked off with the rest of the men. She wasn't the only one. All the women gathered quietly. They watched their loved ones depart with tears in their eyes. Whispers of affection floated through the air. Rose stood beside her, and shed her own tears for Philip, the man she loved. These men didn't deserve the brutal fate that might await them.

More groups of men had joined the Fortune City fighters earlier that morning. The familiar rumble of ATVs sounded as they loaded up weapons and gear. Some men rode motorcycles, machines Rose had introduced her to, and the roar of the engines echoed as they sped away. Once the men had traveled a mile, Selah and Rose made their way to the stables in silence.

Selah wore the clothes Rose had suggested, dark earth tones that blended into the natural environment. Charcoal pants and a dark green tank for her, brown for Rose, both with sturdy hiking boots. They saddled their horses quickly, Rose's chestnut mare, Marble, and her own black steed, Ashland.

Selah glanced back at the town as they mounted up. Some women headed toward the church to pray. Others walked to the shops to distract themselves. Their steps were slow and deliberate, as if any slight disruption would destroy their worlds. A few simply wandered, lost in thought, just as she was. The men were already far beyond the town's borders, and their mission had begun. Selah steeled herself. It was time for them.

They hid their weapons along the horses' flanks and took a route that kept them hidden from the town's view. Once they traveled a safe distance, Rose slowed the pace. They tied their hair back. "Now for the paint," Rose said, pulling out camouflage makeup. "It'll help us blend into the forest."

Selah allowed Rose to paint her, the earthy tones of green and brown covering her hands, face, and neck. She felt ridiculous at first, but if it helped them stay hidden, she'd endure it.

"These will let us hear what the men are saying," Rose handed her a communicator earpiece. "But only press this button if you need to speak." There was a red button on the bottom.

She slipped the earpiece around her right ear, and they continued up the mountain. The plan was simple: follow the men from a distance. Remain hidden by the ridges and trees.

They galloped when the terrain allowed and walked when it didn't. The dense forest around them gave her a sense of peace. Despite everything, despite the danger ahead, the wilderness felt like a sanctuary.

Rose picked up the pace when the ridge flattened. "We need to move faster when we can. We've got horses, but they have ATVs."

Her thoughts drifted to Ian. Every time they passed a landmark she had seen with him on their first journey to Fortune City, she couldn't help but smile. Memories flooded her mind. She never appreciated memories in Atlis, if she had any. There, people faded into the fog and were forgotten. Here, memories were precious, and she clung to them.

They reached the highest peak. Rose pulled out her binoculars. "They're not moving too fast."

Selah heard Ian's voice through the communicator. "I wish this was over."

Vincent's reply was calm, but there was an undercurrent of tension. "Take heart. It will be over before you know it."

The fear in their voices made her heart ache. She didn't want them to be afraid. She gripped the reins tighter, forcing herself to focus. But then Rose suddenly stopped the horses and dismounted. She drew her rifle. Selah followed her lead.

"There's a group of Black Guards down there." Rose said. Her voice was low and steady. "They know the men are coming. It's a trap."

Selah's stomach twisted. "What do we do?"

Rose quickly called Vincent and explained the situation, without revealing their current position. Selah watched through her scope. Her hands trembled slightly as she saw the Black Guard soldiers spread out below. Their black uniforms and helmets blended into the shadows.

Rose ended the call and turned to her. "Okay, Selah, we have to act. Can you—"

"I've got the one on the east side," Selah interrupted and steadied her rifle. She aimed for the small gap between the guard's helmet and mask. With practiced precision, she fired. One by one, the soldiers fell. Twenty, four bodies lay still by the time she lowered her weapon.

Rose stared at her, wide, eyed. "Selah... do you realize what you just did?"

"I protected the men." Selah bluntly replied. There was no regret. The guards would have shown them no mercy.

Vincent's voice crackled through the communicator. "Someone fired a rifle... one of ours."

"Who?" Ian asked.

"I don't know. Another group must've arrived."

She shared a brief, tense smile with Rose, but the humor quickly faded as the weight of the situation settled back in. They mounted their horses and continued along the ridge. The trees casting long shadows in the afternoon sun.

Rose eventually handed her a small vial with a glass pill inside. "In case we're caught," she said quietly. "It's cyanide. If the worst happens, take this instead of letting them make you a breeder. You crunch it with your teeth and death is in a matter of seconds."

She stared at the vial. Death was preferable to becoming a tool for the Monarch. She nodded and slipped it into her pocket.

They rode in silence until Rose abruptly halted again. "I heard something."

Ahead, on the ridge, a sentry tower loomed. Two guards stood inside. Their hands rested on what looked like massive guns.

"We need to take them out," Rose whispered. "You get the one on the east."

They aimed together, Rose counting down. Two shots, two bodies slumped over the weapons. They hurried to the tower. They tied the horses in the underbrush and moving stealthily toward the metal door. Inside, it was eerily quiet. They cleared the lower rooms before climbing the tower.

Rose quickly disabled the alarm system. She severed the cables and muttered under her breath. "We've got some time now. Let's hope no one notices."

She felt a flicker of relief, but it didn't last. She saw more guards emerge into the valley. "They're coming," she whispered

CHAPTER 40

The tunnels shook with the tremors of the core's countermeasure. The turbulence spread through Division T. Lights flickered violently and cast erratic shadows as the hum of the system grew louder, more insistent. Trajan and Marcus pressed on. Their breath was ragged, and their bodies battered. The sound of interminable pursuit closed in behind them.

"We're almost there," Marcus clutched his side where blood seeped through a makeshift bandage. His face was pale. His movements had grown sluggish, but his determination burned in eyes.

"Don't slow down now." Trajan growled. He grabbed Marcus's arm to steady him. "If we don't shut this thing down, nothing else will matter."

The passage opened into a vast chamber beneath the core. The air was thick with the acrid tang of burning circuits. Machinery whirred and hissed; sparks flew in overloaded panels as the system struggled to maintain its rapidly expanding countermeasure.

In the center of the room stood a secondary console. Its surface faintly glowed. It pulsed like a heart, connected to the core above by a web of cables.

"This is it," Marcus muttered. He staggered toward the console. "The access point."

Trajan scanned the chamber, knife in hand. The air felt alive. It crackled with static energy. "We don't have much time. How do we stop it?"

Marcus collapsed onto the console. His hands trembled as he activated the interface. "We have to overload the system. Force it to shut down before it finishes adapting."

"And if it doesn't work?"

Marcus shot him a grim smile. "Then we'll know what it feels like to be vaporized."

The console lit up as Marcus worked. His fingers flew across the holographic display. The room trembled again. The low rumble vibrated through the floor as the countermeasure intensified. Remainders of the guard reached the entrance. Their shadowy forms gathered as they advanced. They couldn't get past the industrial locks holding the door.

Trajan moved to intercept them. His knife flashed as he lunged at the nearest man. He only allowed a couple of pursuers inside, where they fought. Blood spurted as he severed a limb, but the soldiers pressed on, their weapons fired ominously, but uselessly. They had apparently forgone their weapons training. He dodged an angry bullet. The heat singed his arm as he countered with a powerful strike to another drone's chest plate.

"Marcus!" he shouted. His voice hoarse over the din of battle. "Whatever you're doing, do it faster!"

"Working on it!" Marcus snapped. His voice warbled. Blood dripped onto the console and stained the glowing interface as his movements slowed. He clutched his side, his breathing labored. "I... I need you to finish this."

Trajan's heart sank. "What are you talking about?"

Marcus turned to him. His face was pale but his gaze fierce. "I'll guide you. You're faster than me now. Just... trust me."

Trajan hesitated for a heartbeat, then nodded. He ensured the door wouldn't open back up. He sprinted to the console. His knife was slick with muck and blood. Marcus leaned against the edge. His voice barely audible as he explained the commands.

"Override the failsafe here..." Marcus pointed to a glowing panel. "Then—then reroute the power surge into the countermeasure. It'll... collapse the adaptation cycle."

He followed instructions. His hands moved with precision he didn't know he had. The drones pressed closer, and he felt the heat of their weapons scorching the air around him.

"It's working," Marcus whispered. He slumped to the floor. "Keep going."

As the final command entered the system, the countermeasure began to falter. The hum of the machinery grew uneven. Its rhythm was broken as the lights dimmed. Trajan glanced at Marcus. His friend's body was weak, but his eyes still burned with resolve.

A horrifying slow clap echoed through the chamber. It chilled Trajan to his core. He spun around to see Nero emerge from the shadows. His gaudy robes glinted in the flickering light. His face was a mask of triumph. His laughter was sharp and cruel.

"Well done," Nero said. His voice dripped with mockery. "I couldn't have orchestrated this better myself."

Trajan's grip on his knife tightened. "What the hell are you talking about?"

Nero stepped closer. His leisurely movements reminded him of a predator toying with its prey. "You've done exactly what I wanted. The Countermeasure was never meant to protect the Monarch. It was meant to purge the Representatives... and the drones."

Trajan's blood ran cold. "Purge?"

Nero grinned. His teeth gleamed. "The representatives fled, of course. Cowards. But the drones won't care. And when the Representatives are gone, the colonies will be mine."

"Yours?" Trajan spat. "You're insane."

"Am I?" Nero spread his arms. His expression one of mock innocence. "The Monarch is a relic, a machine past its prime. The Representatives are parasites. But me? I'll be the Emperor. Not just of a division, but of all of them. The colonies need a true leader."

"You're no leader," Trajan growled. "You're just another tyrant."

"Tyrants make history." Nero's laughter rang out again. It echoed through the chamber. He opened his mouth to respond, but the words never came. A figure emerged from the shadows, maybe a drone, silent and deliberate. Its hand gripped a knife, and in one swift motion, it plunged the blade into Nero's back.

His eyes widened in shock as he fell to his knees. The drone stepped back. His face was blank. His movements were precise. Nero collapsed. His laughter replaced by choking gasps.

Trajan stared, stunned. "How...?"

Marcus chuckled weakly from the floor. "I told you... drones aren't as lifeless as they seem."

Trajan rushed to Marcus's side. His heart pounded. Marcus's face was pale, his breathing shallow, but he managed a weak smile. "We did it," Marcus whispered. "The Countermeasure stopped it."

Trajan nodded and gripped his friend's hand tightly. "We did." He smiled back, but the same unspoken question plagued his mind. At what cost?

The core's hum began to fade above them. Its lights dimmed as the system shut down. The Monarch was broken. Its grip on the colony shattered. But the Representatives were gone, the drones awakened, and the future was uncertain.

Trajan looked at Marcus, his voice quiet. "What now?"

Marcus closed his eyes, his smile faint. "Now... we rest."

CHAPTER 41

The Black Guards moved with precision, dark figures cutting through the misty gloom. Their approach sent a jolt through Selah's chest. She and Rose pulled back, pressing themselves against the cold concrete lip. The rough surface bit into Selah's skin, but she barely registered the sensation. Her pulse pounded in her ears, each beat louder than the last.

She forced herself to breathe. Forced herself to still the tremble that threatened to betray them.

A knock, soft, deliberate, sounded from below.

She clenched her teeth against the fear clawing up her throat. Too soon. It had to be a trap. Yet Rose, moving cautiously, edged toward the narrow window and peered through.

A breathless pause. Then, Rose whispered, "It's Ian and Vincent."

Relief hit Selah so fast her knees almost gave way. She grabbed a nearby shelf to avoid falling down.

They unlatched the door and pulled the men inside. Vincent first, grinning, eyes sharp with recognition. Then Ian, his expression unreadable.

"I knew it was you," Vincent said, voice tinged with quiet triumph. "Knew those shots belonged to us."

She didn't speak. She couldn't. Ian stepped toward her. His gaze heavy with unspoken words. He took her by the arm and pulled her aside.

"You weren't honest with me."

A lump formed in her throat. She struggled to swallow it down. "I couldn't be." Her voice cracked. Tears burned at the edges of her vision, but she refused to let them fall. "I had to be here."

Ian exhaled sharply, then he whispered softer, "I know."

Without another word, he pulled her into a tight embrace. His warmth, his solid weight, grounded her for just a moment. The tension unraveled, briefly, fleetingly, before the world outside tore it apart.

Gunfire erupted in the valley below. A sudden burst of chaos.

Ian pulled back. Vincent's grin faded. The moment shattered. No hesitation. No time for second thoughts. They moved. Vincent and Ian rushed toward the stairwell, weapons drawn, their footsteps lost beneath the rising thunder of battle.

Her stomach clenched as she watched him disappear into the violence. Dread settled over her like a lead weight.

She and Rose remained behind. The tower offered an advantage, a view of the battlefield through the monitors lining the far wall. A false sense of safety. But safety meant nothing when the world below crumbled.

Selah leaned in. Her eyes scanned the flickering feeds. The men battled through the valley. They darted between boulders and tree trunks. Smoke curled like tendrils around their movements. Every gunshot sent a jolt through her bones.

Then, the ground shuddered. A low, groaning tremor, as if something beneath the earth had begun to wake. She grabbed the table for balance. "An earthquake?" Her voice came out smaller than she intended.

Rose's breath hitched. "No, no." She shook her head. "This is something else."

The flickering camera feeds glitched in and out. The screen closest to Selah froze, then snapped back to life, just in time to show the first buildings collapse.

A wave of destruction surged through Atlis.

Concrete split like brittle glass. Towers toppled, one after another. The streets buckled and tore apart like fragile fabric. The drones, the mindless, the controlled, walked straight into the devastation without a moment's hesitation.

Her heart stopped.

Vincent's voice crackled through the communicator, barely audible over the chaos. "They've detonated the city...."

She couldn't breathe. Couldn't move. His last phrase before be cut out: "Atlis is gone."

The words settled in her chest, suffocating, inescapable. Everything she had known, everything that once stood, collapsed before her eyes.

Atlis was dead.

CHAPTER 42

Trajan stood amidst the shattered remnants of the colony's grand atrium. Its former elegance now buried beneath ruin. The skeletal remains of its infrastructure loomed around him, silent and forsaken.

Faint, flickering lights cast jagged shadows that stretched like phantoms across the scorched walls. Fractured support beams hung at unnatural angles, groaning under their own weight, threatening collapse.

From severed cables above, molten sparks rained down. They hissed as they met pools of stagnant water. The scent of charred metal, burnt circuitry, and something far more acrid clung to the air, heavy and suffocating. Each breath carried the taste of finality.

His boots crunched over the brittle remnants of the past, glass shards, splintered stone, the discarded fragments of what had once been lives. The sound echoed in the emptiness, the only noise left in a place that once teemed with voices, movement, purpose.

No one remained.

He tried to comprehend the massacre, but no clarity came. The Representatives' final decree, had it truly been so ruthless? Had they, in their retreat, ensured that no one, not emperor, not drone, could seize their power? Or had this been something else? The countermeasure.

A deep unease settled in his chest. Had it been his doing?

The AXIOM. Every citizen bore one, embedded beneath the skin, an unbreakable tether to their rulers. They once served as identification, as compliance enforcement, as tracking devices, but now, they had become weapons.

The detonation left nothing behind but silence. No warning. No struggle. No time to resist. Every marked body, collapsed where it had stood.

He had seen executions before. He had witnessed systematic purges, the cold efficiency of power wiping away undesirables as if they had never existed. But this... this had not been a culling. This had been annihilation.

He moved through the ruins in a daze. Every step guided by muscle memory rather than thought. His chest felt hollow, his pulse a distant rhythm, detached and meaningless. *Alone now.* The last living being in a kingdom of the dead.

Time lost its shape. The silence pressed against him and grew heavier with each minute. It seeped into his bones. A weight beyond grief, beyond guilt.

His path led him to the colony's outermost wall, where the looming barriers still stood. They cast their oppressive presence over the remains of the fallen city. They had once seemed impenetrable. They had once felt eternal. Now, they stood as relics of a system that no longer existed.

With nothing left inside, movement became effortless. No checkpoints. No patrols. No overseers.

No one left to stop him.

He halted at the main gates, their metal surface scorched, buckled in places, yet still standing. Beyond them, the remains of one of the colony's towering structures jutted into the sky, skeletal and crumbling. A final monument to what once was.

The air felt thinner here. Colder. Sharp against his skin. For so long, he envisioned the world beyond these walls as a barren wasteland. A place of desolation, of ruin, of slow death. Now, he understood. The true wasteland had been inside.

Beyond the gates, movement stirred in the distance. Faint figures against the dying light. He narrowed his eyes and watched them.

They were apparently human. A question clawed at the edges of his mind: Enemies? Outsiders? Survivors?

He didn't know. He had no strength left to fear. No purpose left to defend. He exhaled and watched his breath coil into the cold air. He had no choice but to move forward.

So he stepped through the gates and approached them, hoping, though he dared not believe, they weren't here to end what little remained of him.

CHAPTER 43

They located one survivor. A man draped in filth and shadows, barely more than a husk, yet his voice carried a certainty that defied his condition. An emperor, he claimed. She had never heard of emperors, but that meant nothing in the colony. So much of the world remained unknown, locked away in databases she would never access, in histories rewritten or erased entirely.

Drones held no knowledge beyond what they received. Outside those walls, they might as well have been children, conditioned, obedient, unquestioning. They lived in obedient ignorance because ignorance ensured obedience.

Efforts began at once to strip the ruins for anything of value. To repurpose what remained for those who still endured beyond the colonies. They had expected a battle. They had braced for an extended war, one requiring patience, strategy, and sacrifice. Yet in the end, resistance never came. Only fire. Only silence.

The man called himself Trajan. The last to draw breath behind those once, impenetrable walls. She never believed the Order would truly purge every soul within. Every single one.

No victory cries rang out. No exhilaration swelled among them. Relief? Perhaps. An absence of tension, a breath finally exhaled. But nothing more. No thrill in what had been done. The Monarch had prepared them for combat, not this, this eradication.

She had steeled herself for something greater than a slaughter. The sheer finality unsettled her. An entire civilization, reduced to nothing in an instant. No struggle. No exchange. Just an execution, disguised as inevitability.

She had been born to serve the Monarch. Bred to serve the Monarch. All ways belonged to the Monarch. All thoughts, the Monarch's thoughts. She had sworn eternal loyalty to the entity that knew all things past, all things present, and all things yet to come.

And she would not stop until it fell.

Damn the Monarch.

About the Author:

L. Chambers Wright, who also writes as Laura Wright, has spent a lifetime crafting stories that bridge the gap between the real and the uncanny. With publishing credits spanning nearly every genre, from poetry to nonfiction, her work is as diverse as it is captivating. Raised on the eerie whispers of Appalachian folklore and ghost stories, she weaves the chilling, the mysterious, and the forgotten into her writing, ensuring that legends never truly fade. You can find more of her work at Laurawrites.net.